A Fool in Time

MIKE GIRARD

A FOOL IN TIME
Copyright © 2019 Mike Girard
ISBN-13: 9781705363584
Edited by Lloyd L. Corricelli
Cover Art by Daniel Batal
Cover Design by Lloyd L. Corricelli
Proofed by Ginny Rudis, Lisa Z, and Rick Kilbashian (Skillet).

Available Now at Amazon & Other Fine Booksellers

PREFACE

It's been my experience that people don't usually read a preface. They might skim through it, but unless they see the words SECRET TREASURE MAP LOCATION, they're onto chapter one.

But please take a minute to read this one that I may properly set up the story you're about to read. I wrote a book a few years back called "Psycho Chicken and Other Foolish Tales." It recounted the story of my band, The Fools, from its beginning in the late 70's in the small coal mining town of Ipswich, Massachusetts, to its continuance in the present day. While I may have taken some liberties with the Truth, I will stand by what my guitar player, Rich Bartlett, said after reading the book:

"The story is pretty much true, even if the details aren't."

Ah well, tomato, tomahto.

This book, while telling some Fools based stories, will be more of a personal accounting of my travels and adventures, both before and during my time with the band. In prepping for this book I reread the first one and noticed that there were large periods of time that were skipped over. Much like the missing years of Jesus between thirteen and thirty-three, I too left gaping holes in my story.

And now for the SECRET TREASURE MAP LOCATION! (Sorry, I'm just trying to hang onto your attention)

For those of you who haven't read the first book, you can find it on Amazon or at one my shows with The Fools or Mike Girard's Big Swinging Things. The *Boston*

Globe called it a 'hoot'...is there any higher praise? Hopefully this book will stand alone, but if you need more, that's a good place to start.

I should mention a word about the artwork you'll find in this book. I considered hiring a professional artist, but in my own whimsical way thought it might be more fun for you to see things through my eyes. The problem is I'm a storyteller, not a visual artist...hence the drawings that look like they were done by a Fourth grader.

Finally, I need to thank my family, both real, extended and imagined, for their support and encouragement, and my bandmates for their indulgence. All of you have made this story possible, if not probable.

And now, let's saunter back through time...

Mike Girard
From the Fools Mansion
October 3, 2019

FOREWORD

When Mike asked me to write the foreword for his new book, I initially declined; primarily because I'm not really much of a writer and better known as a poet. After much thought and communing with Dionysus, I couldn't get the vision of his disappointed face out of my mind. I finally agreed with one caveat; he could never tell anyone who actually wrote this forward. You may be able to guess after reading this book, but only Mike will ever know the truth.

This story is one of my Foolish friend and his incredible journey of growth and discovery. I first met Mike in the late Sixties and found him to be a bright and sparkly young man. We shared a very close moment with an odd friend of mine and then went our separate ways. Oddly enough however, we kept crossing paths and at first I admit I found it to be an annoyance, but in time we eventually grew to become compadres.

My personal thoughts on Mike at this point are best put to verse:

A shiny sparkly lad, his eyes clear and bright
His voice shimmers amongst the gods of old and new
Who is this child of song and time I see before my face?
Son to the brave warrior who set us all free
Brother to the mime who killed the eagle with the golden voice
Husband to his muse, a woman of dignity and grace

Fuck the vinyl corporate demons of the old ways
Their ears bleed to the vibrations of their ignorance
His fans know the truth is held in the music
A warrior in sound, in this time and many others
A traveler who has learned Gaia's secrets
And most importantly, the secret that the spirit survives

I hope you enjoy this journey through time and life with Mike. I know I loved every minute of our journey together...except one...but that's a story for another time.

JM *aka* TLK
From an undisclosed time and place

**This book is dedicated
to my wife Ginny &
my daughter Sara.**

**Even if time travel enabled it,
I wouldn't change a thing.**

The Intrepid Author somewhere in time...

1

Once Upon a Time

"Time is what keeps everything from happening at once."
Ray Cummings

I was eight years old and it was winter, but I was walking with my Dad and I was carrying the Axe! No this is not the beginning of a slasher movie, it's a kid walking with his dad on the way to cut down a Christmas tree. The reason for the capital letter Axe is that we had a crowded family and I didn't get to spend too much alone time with my Dad, never mind carry the weapon of tree destruction. It made me feel like a big kid.

We headed out back of our house and made our way through a field on towards the thick forest in the distance. I knew the property belonged to the millionaire who lived in a mansion in the midst of a few hundred acres of woodland. His name was Patrick Westlake, and he was a bit of a mysterious figure. This was well before Google, so to call him mysterious was to simply say that we didn't know how he'd come by his millions. The rumor was that he had some showbiz connection, but this may have rested solely on the fact that he'd purchased the estate a few years earlier from the previous owner, Hollywood actor Raymond Massey; best known for his role in 'Arsenic & Old Lace.'

I knew these woods quite well as they were the go to adventure destination for me and my two best friends, Stacey Pedrick and Brian Farina. (Yes that Stacey Pedrick, the longtime Fools guitar player). The three of us spent hours in these woods; capturing flags, hiding and seeking, climbing trees, and partaking in our favorite past time...spying on the millionaire.

Any detective worth his badge knows that if you want to learn anything about a neighborhood, ask the young boys who live there. They know whose dad is the grouchiest, whose mom is squabbling with which neighbor, and which yard can be run through with the least amount of risk and they are so willing to gossip about it all.

Though we didn't know much about Mr. Westlake, we did know that he had a chauffeur, that he liked to ride horses, and that he liked music. These things we learned from high above his property, looking down from the elms and the oaks. Tree climbing is a core part of childhood; climbing up where the birds and squirrels are, and looking down on a world from which you can feel temporarily separated is exhilarating.

My Dad, of course, didn't know about my investigative adventures, and I volunteered nothing about them as we walked along. Oddly enough, it didn't occur to me that we were about to poach a tree off of someone else's property. After all, there were thousands of them all around us.

We were just agreeing on the benefits of a small six foot tree, and about to clear away the brush underneath

it so as to begin the cutting, when we heard the distinctive sound of a horse coming up behind us...a horse with a rider.

"Well hello there," Patrick Westlake said, as if he was stumbling upon old friends at the super market.

His big horse snorted to a stop and he slipped easily off and stood in front of my Dad with his hand out.

"Patrick Westlake," he said.

My first impression, upon seeing him up close, was that he could have just stepped out of a cowboy movie. Not that he was dressed that way, it was more his look and manner; tall and athletic, not unattractive, but certainly not Hollywood handsome. It was something about the look in his eye, as if he was about to share a joke.

"I'm sorry, sir," my Dad said. "We're trespassing and we shouldn't be here."

"Nonsense," Westlake said, "I was just thinking that there are so many great Christmas trees in this forest, and I'm the only one who gets to use them. Take what you want, but not before telling me your name."

They talked for a bit and my Dad relaxed to the point where they seemed like old friends. After this meeting my Dad would describe Westlake to his friends as being 'salt of the earth.' It was my Dad's highest compliment.

The other thing I remember from that day was Westlake turning to me and saying, "And who's this curious young fellow?"

At that moment I knew in a way that I can't explain, that he was aware that my friends and I had been spying on him. The other thing I remember is him watching and even helping us take down the tree, after which he nodded to my Dad, and then looked at me and said, "I guess we'll be seeing each other again."

And he was right.

2

Into the Mystic

"When I was younger I could remember anything, whether it happened or not"
Mark Twain

I was a happy kid, in spite of my underperforming eyeballs that left me with very thick glasses. I soon got used to the 'Coke bottle' comments that I heard from just about every eight year old comedian, but after a while it didn't bother me. Though I was small for my age, I was athletic and sports came easy to me. Not that I was very good at anything (except running fast), it's more that I was fairly coordinated and competitive and I learned the rules of whatever game in order to play.

The 'running fast' part of my early life had much to do with the fact that I was apparently an irritating pain in the ass to most everyone who came into contact with me. Though I didn't see it that way, the following commentaries are hard to ignore:

"So we would get to high school early if we could, and hit the gym, and this day someone decided to push the trampoline under the basket so that we could jump and stuff the ball. I bounced too far under the rim and pogoed a couple times up against the rim. I wasn't hurt bad but the Doc shaved my head and the stitches

were quite visible. The little bastard called me 'baseball' and the name stuck. It's a good thing for him I couldn't catch him."
Anonymous

"He used to let me copy his homework in history class, but one day I copied it and my paper says shit like 'Genghis Khan was the 14th President.' Yes funny, but I failed the fucking class."
Hatlo Freebus

"I don't know him, but I'm guessing he's a dick."
Man on the street

I didn't think I was being a pain in the ass, I thought I was being funny. Therein lies the problem, as a playwright once kind of said; one man's joke is often another man's misery. And through all of it my fleetness of foot served me well, as I ran from upper classmen, insane adults, and even, on occasion, upset relatives.

Through it all I started to learn where the comedy line was...the one you don't cross, unless you're ready to run as fast as you can. And I became a huge fan of that era's novelty records. Where I grew up in the greater Boston area, you could hear an amazing array of novelty stuff on WMEX. DJ Arnie 'Woo Woo' Ginsburg played everything from Lonney Donnigan's *'Does your Chewing Gum Lose its Flavor'* to *'Tie Me Kangaroo Down'* by Rolf Harris. Mixed in with this were such other nuggets from the black community such as *'I Put a Spell on You'* by Screamin' J. Hawkins, and *'Say Man'* by Bo Diddley. There was also *'Alley Oop'* by the

Hollywood Argyles, and 'Charlie Brown' by the Coasters.

I learned them all by heart and sang them on the school bus to whoever would listen. I wasn't trying to be a singer back then, it was just funny stuff that I was trying to copy. Years later we Fools were honored to have more than one of our tunes make Dr. Demento's playlist. Demento was responsible for breaking novelty acts like Weird Al Yankovich and for years had a nationally syndicated show that played nothing but novelty songs.

It was during the summer after the Christmas tree altercation that one Saturday morning I ended up alone with no one to hang with. Stacey and Brian were both busy with whatever, and I didn't feel like connecting out of the blue with my second tier of (sort of) friends so I did what the three of us would have done and headed out back towards the woods. It may not be as much fun to climb a tree and spy alone, but it was better than doing nothing.

It was a perfect July day; hot, and with that clear summer air and no clouds in the sky that made you think you could see for miles. As I walked into the shade of the woods the temperature cooled a bit and I moved quietly through the trees. There was a sound in the air that soon became a song as I walked towards the mansion. It wasn't unusual to hear music in these woods. Westlake apparently liked music and played it loudly. Rock n' roll, blues, country, and classical all occasionally emanated from his mansion.

As I got closer, I recognized the song. It was "Charlie Brown" by the Coasters, with its reoccurring line, "he's

gonna' get caught, just you wait and see...why's everybody always picking on me?" It was one of my personal favorites and I almost laughed out loud when I recognized it.

We had three different trees in the midst of the dense forest that surrounded his house that we liked to climb. Our favorite was an eighty foot elm. Not only was it a perfect climbing tree, but it gave us a great view of the back of his house. The mansion was three stories tall and horseshoe shaped, and it supposedly had about fifty rooms, give or take. My view, from halfway up the elm, was of the back yard; the area between the two arms of the horseshoe. In the middle of that large area was a huge fountain, surrounded by a stone patio.

As I sat on a limb watching, I readied myself for the possibility that no one would emerge from the house, but it was a beautiful day, and I was high up in a tree, so I was happy. I was about to either climb down or fall asleep when I saw two men carrying a large wooden chair out into the patio, followed by Westlake. They placed the chair in front of the fountain. It looked a bit like a simple throne, but it was almost a bit too large for normal sized people. The three men stood there waiting for a moment when Westlake looked at his watch and said, "Here he comes."

The next part is what I've spent years trying to figure out. There was a slight sparkle of light in the air around the chair, and then there was someone sitting in it who hadn't been there seconds before. I didn't get the best look at the person in the chair because I made a loud gasping noise of surprise, and much to my shock, Westlake turned and looked directly up at me.

I went down that tree as fast as I'd ever tried to go down any tree, probably dangerously so, and dropped the last six feet with my feet already in a dead run...and ran full into Patrick Westlake.

"Ah, Charlie Brown I presume," he said with a smile, at the same time preventing me from falling down. He towered over me, and perhaps sensing my terror, he went down on one knee.

"I...I....didn't see anything," I blurted out.

He barked one loud laugh and said, "I'm glad you like climbing my trees. I've forgotten how much fun that must be." As he was still down on a knee, and smiling that funny smile, I lost my fear and felt almost at ease.

"We like climbing them," I said, only then realizing I had just incriminated my two best friends.

"Ah yes," he said. "You and your two buddies."

He didn't say it at all as an accusation, it was more an acknowledgement of something we both knew. And before I had time to make up some defense of it all, he stood up and said, "I don't know about you but I'm really thirsty. Let's get something." With that he headed toward his house and I followed.

"Hannah!" he yelled loudly. "We have a guest, bring cookies and milk!" As we walked onto his stone patio, I couldn't help but look at the big wooden chair. It looked really old, but sturdy.

"That chair is ancient but we'll talk about that some other time. It's hot out here so let's go inside."

We walked in and sat at a small country table in the middle of a large kitchen. That's when I met the first maid I've encountered before or since. Hannah was beautiful, and of an age I couldn't determine, but what did I know, I was eight. She too had a certain smile, and like his, it was disarming. As a young boy, I was used to adults talking over me, or mostly ignoring me, but these two acted as if I would momentarily do or say something clever. Only my best friends treated me that way.

Over the course of milk and cookies, and the next hour, Westlake and I talked about Ipswich, about music, about television shows, and about my thoughts on all sorts of things. It was new ground for me, being taken seriously, and I realized that I was being careful about how I said things. I wanted my answers to be how I really felt.

Yes, Jan and Dean were ok, but weren't they just a second rate version of the Beach Boys.

My Dad loves Frank Sinatra, but I think Dean Martin is the best.

Barney Fife is the funniest guy on TV.

My friend Brian just got this thing called a skateboard. It came from California and it's like surfing on the sidewalk.

Those were some of my deep thoughts.

Through it all he seemed interested and amused, and I even learned some stuff about him. He'd traveled a lot, but he really liked Ipswich. No, he didn't have a connection to Hollywood, but he had purchased this property because of the history surrounding it.

And then he said this: "I've got some work around here that needs doing and maybe you're the right person for the job."

"Um, what job?" I mumbled.

"Well we'd have to clear it with your parents, and we're only talking a couple days a week, when weather and school allow."

"What job?"

"Here's what I'm thinking," he said. "I've got a lot of trees. I've got elm and birch and oak, and so many others, but I'd really like to know HOW many and of what type. So what I'd like you to do is count my trees."

"Huh?"

"I want you to count my trees," he repeated. "I know you like climbing them, and occasionally cutting one down, so how'd you like to count them?" His eyes were smiling, but I knew he was serious.

I thought for a minute and said, "Sure."

That's how my job as a tree counter started. But the other thing I remember about that day was this: As I was about to leave, he asked me simply, "are you going to tell your buddies about the chair?"

Even though Brian and Stacey and I told each other everything about everything, I thought about it for a brief minute and said, "No." And I knew I meant it. And I've kept that promise until today.

3

Counting Trees

*"As the poet said, 'only God can make a tree',
probably because it's so hard to put the bark on."*
Woody Allen

*"A brief explanation of an acorn---in a nutshell it's
an oak tree"*
Anonymous

I know what you're probably thinking; that he gave me
the job to keep me from spying on him. After all, what
fun is it to spy on a property if you pretty much have the
run of the place a couple days a week? That thought
didn't occur to me until much later. At the time, my
eight year old brain decided that a very important man
had given me a very important job, and I took my
position of Tree Counter very seriously.

Selling my parents on the gig wasn't that hard; my
Mom was a little confused by it, but my Dad said
something like, "who knows what millionaires think is
important?" As if the brains of millionaires were
fashioned from some exotic materials. Also, since my
Dad had already decided Westlake was 'salt of the
earth'...and because a visit to the mansion with me in
tow would be needed, it became a done deal.

At an appointed time, Dad and I hopped in the car and drove down the street and through the front gates of the estate. This time we were not sneaking through the woods like peasants! No, we were driving up the goddam road like people who were invited, because goddam it we were! I could tell my father was impressed as we made the final turn into the circle that brought us to the front of the place. "Wow," he said.

It was hard not to be impressed; the front was imposing. I was to later learn that it was based on a Seventeenth century Stuart style mansion; but to my young eyes it was all brick and chimneys, fronted by two enormous crouching lions, one on either side of the entry way. If any enemies showed up made of stone, the stone lions would protect you.

Leaning against one of the lions, in an untucked shirt and dungarees was our host. He walked toward our car as my Dad parked, and was at his side as we got out.

"Mike," he said, "welcome" and shook Dad's hand.

"Mr. Westlake," my Dad said.

"Call me Pat," he said.

Wow, I thought...Pat and Mike. It was after this meeting that my Dad began to foster the dream of quitting the coal mines and working as an estate manager for Westlake but he would keep that to himself for years.

As we walked into the mansion he nodded at me, and at first I was irritated that he didn't shake my hand and welcome me. After a minute though, I realized that it was both of us welcoming my Dad to this place.

We walked past the grand staircase and into the ballroom. Westlake paused and looked around at the enormous room and said, "It's just all too big...let's go out back."

We walked through to the back patio where Hannah had put out sandwiches and Cokes atop a picnic table near the fountain. The big chair was nowhere in sight. I don't remember much else about that morning except that it went well, and soon after I was a gainfully employed tree counter.

And so for the rest of that summer, up until school started, I would spend two days a week, four hours a day on his property counting trees. For this I was payed the sum of ten dollars a week. Not a lot of money by today's standards, but let's remember, back then gas only cost ten cents a gallon. Ok, I'm lying about that (and only that) but it seemed like a fortune to me.

So how does a tree counter count trees? Westlake had it all worked out for me the first day I showed up. It went like this: He handed me a clipboard and on it were ten different colors and next to each was an associated tree. So oak was yellow, elm was green, maple was blue and so on. I was to pick a starting spot and work my way counter-clockwise around his vast property, always keeping the mansion to my left and the boundary of his property to the right. How would I know which tree was which? He came with me to the starting spot and tacked three different oak trees with yellow ribbons.

"That's what an oak tree looks like," he said. "You can count all of them around the edge of the property, then work your way slowly in. Use a yellow ribbon periodically so you'll know how wide a swath you're working. It's going to take you a while to count all the trees, but for starters, just do the oaks."

It did take me a while. Working four hours a day, two days a week it took me the rest of that summer and part of the next to count the oaks. As to my friends, Stacey and Brian, when Westlake said that they could visit me and have a look around, the place almost instantly became boring to them; no longer a forbidden fruit.

My favorite part of the job was Hannah visiting me every work day to bring me a snack, during which time I would ask her, in that endless way children have, lots of questions.

"Is he married?" (No) "Does he have a girlfriend?" (Probably) "You don't know?" (He's away a lot, and besides, I don't pry). She said this last bit with an eyebrow raised in my direction, an inference that was totally lost on me. In retrospect, I'm sure that her daily visits were part of the deal made with my parents...keep an eye on little Michael.

One other thing of note from that early period; both she and Westlake didn't call me Michael, they called me Mike. It's hard to explain the affect that had on me. Maybe it was that Mike sounded somehow more rugged than Michael, the skinny little kid with thick glasses. As Mike, I walked the forest a little more confidently, a young man with a purpose.

Occasionally, but not often, Westbrook would bring the snack, at which point I would ask him questions about Hannah. "Is she married?" (No) "Does she have a boyfriend?" (Maybe) "Where's she from?" (She's...not from around here). The way he paused when he answered that last question seemed curious, but then so much about them was.

I wanted to ask him about the man who appeared in the chair, who he was, and what kind of magic had brought that about. And who were the two men carrying the chair? But all I could muster was a general question that I must have thought would catch him off guard.

"So where'd you get that chair?" I asked off handedly.

Without answering, or missing a beat he said, "Someday we'll get to that, but for now, you've got quite a few more trees to count."

So I did, getting more done during summer vacations, and less after school during the spring and fall. Westlake was often away for extended periods of time, but the work went on, overseen by Hannah.

Soon enough I was in middle school, playing sports, having crushes on girls, and being totally impressed with Stacey, who could now play guitar, and Brian, who could play drums and sing really well. They started a group called the Islanders, and by the time we all got to high school they were playing teen dances and parties. When they practiced at Stacey's, I would sometimes overcome my fears and sing an Animals tune, or some other big hit of the day, but generally, that was something only done in front of best friends (for more info on this period read *Psycho Chicken and other Foolish Tales* available at Amazon.com...It will cost about as much as a large pizza, but even if you're a fast reader, it will last longer).

Through all my life changes, through first romances and first broken hearts, I counted trees; red maple, sugar maple, barberry, chestnut, and birch were all located and counted. Hickory, pine, spruce, black walnut, aspen, willow, and elm, were all tallied and accounted for.

Soon enough it was senior year and by some odd coincidence, I had counted most of the trees on the property. I say coincidence because a number of things ended and began all in the space of a few months. I'd got it into my head that once the tree counting was completed, I'd be asked to undertake some other task, like maybe counting the blades of grass on the front lawn, or the number of pebbles in the driveway. I learned otherwise about a week prior to my graduation. Westlake visited me as I was nearing my last half acre of counting the barberries, a tree really no one cares about. He seemed a bit solemn as he approached, though maybe that's just how my memory has shaped it.

"So, it's down to this then, a few more barberries and you're done. You've done a fine job and it's been a pleasure to have you work here," he said, reaching out to shake my hand.

I was confused and almost pulled my hand back.

"Huh?" I mumbled. "There must be something else."

In all the time I'd worked for him, the conversations we'd had were of a wide range of subjects; music, sports, women, or in my case girls, history (his favorite topic) and politics (my least favorite topic). The one thing we never talked about was what I would do after the counting ended. He gave me a steady look and seemed to come to a decision.

"Let's head back to the house," he said. He never called it The Mansion.

"But I've still got some barberries to count," I protested. I didn't want it to be over.

"That's alright," he said, turning to walk back toward the house. "Even I don't care about barberries."

We walked back in silence, me feeling a great sadness and wondering if I'd done something wrong. When we got to the courtyard he motioned me towards the picnic table. I sat down and he paced a bit in front of me before he began.

"Mike, I value loyalty and friendship above all other things, so my highest compliment to you is to say that you've been a loyal friend, and I'll miss our conversations. I'm going to be leaving here for probably a very long time and..."

"But I could work for Hannah," I said, interrupting him, and trying to forestall what I could tell was the inevitable.

"Actually," he said, "Hannah will be coming with me."

"But who'll be here to run things?" I thought for a moment about pitching him myself for the job, but I knew I was woefully underqualified.

"After a lot of thought I've decided that your dad is the right man for the job. He and I have also become friends. Now please, act surprised tonight, because he's very excited to tell you all."

I pondered this for a moment and said," I could help him."

Westlake smiled and slowly shook his head.

"My young friend," he paused finding the words, "as much as your father would love that, what happens if in a few years I sell this place? Would you go to work in the mines then? You've got to get out of this town and see some of the world. It's a pretty amazing place."

I sat there feeling defeated. And then he said the most curious thing to me.

"I could have made you forget that years ago...there are ways, but then here we are. I've been thinking of how to reward your service and to also give you a graduation present." He paused and walked over near the fountain.

"Ok, Alex, it's time," he said raising his voice.

From within the house, two men appeared carrying a large chair, a chair I hadn't seen for almost ten years. They placed it facing the fountain. I realized that I was barely breathing, but I couldn't help but walk towards it.

"Mike, this is Alex," Westlake said.

The slightly built man with a shock of red hair gave me a nod and a half smile. For some reason, he reminded me of someone from a Lewis Carrol novel.

"And this is John," Westlake added, motioning to the second man.

John also nodded at me. He was much larger than Alex and rougher looking with hands that told me he was a laborer. I'd seen his type all over our little mining town. I thought back and tried to remember; were these the two I'd seen years ago?

Westlake stood behind the chair with his hands on the back of it. The two men stood deferentially off to the side as he spoke to me.

"Have you ever wondered what it would be like to travel back in time...to visit places or events...to view a piece of history as a visitor, and see it from your current perspective?" Westlake asked.

I stood there, my mouth hanging open, unsure what to say.

"I want you to stop for a moment and think of some past event you'd like to see with your own eyes. It's been my experience that the quicker you decide, the more rewarding your experience will be."

"Anywhere? Anytime?" I asked. "We could go see dinosaurs?"

"Perhaps," he replied with a laugh. "Wherever you decide to go, know that I will be there with you, and you'll be totally safe. I would, however, suggest against choosing any event or piece of history that may involve violence."

"So no dinosaurs?"

He ignored my question and continued. "Now I know that this is a lot to digest, so let's sit for a while and drink a beer and I'll try and answer your questions. Also, if you decide that you have no interest in taking such a trip, for whatever reason, the only thing you'll remember about today is that I surprisingly offered you a beer."

Hannah appeared and placed a small iced bucket of beer on the picnic table and I suddenly realized that my childhood had just come to an end.

4

The Wayback Machine

"Music is moonlight in the gloomy night of life."
Jean Paul

"When I was a little boy I told my Dad when I grow up I want to be a musician. My Dad said," You can't do both son."
Chet Atkins

I sat at the picnic table, across from Westlake and Hannah, with a cold bottle of beer in my hand and thought about what I'd just been told. Back when I was an eight year old seeing magic from a tree, I'd thought it was just that. So today had Westlake shown me another amazing thing and said *'abra- kadabra,'* I would have been at ease with the idea that he was secretly a world class magician; at least to me. I looked at the two of them and realized that they were both totally at ease, in spite of what I'd just been told. Somehow it relaxed me enough to take a deep breath.

"I don't know what to think about you two," I said barely above a whisper. "Who are you?"

They both looked at each other and almost giggled, and then looked back at me, sort of like proud parents.

"I know this is hard for you," Westlake said, "but we think you can handle it. Why don't you start asking me questions? It might help you relax."

"There's no way we would let any of this hurt you," Hannah said.

"So years ago that was a time traveler that showed up in that chair?" I almost shouted it.

"Yes," he said.

"Who was he?"

"He's a friend, but does it matter who he was? Aren't you more curious about the how rather than the who?" Westlake asked.

"How does it work," I finally asked, and drank a deep pull of my beer. It wasn't my first beer. Stacey and I and Brian had had more than a couple in high school, usually procured by someone older. This was however my first beer with adults.

Westlake leaned back a bit and looked off into the distance and said this:

"I've been very fortunate in life. Though my parents died when I was young, I was raised by very loving grandparents. They were quite wealthy and gave me every benefit and sent me to the finest schools. Like you, I was a curious fellow and followed my nose to curious places."

I nodded and drank some of my beer. Hannah smiled as she listened to a story she no doubt knew intimately. I felt I was among friends. Westlake continued.

"While at university, I began attending the classes of an eccentric scientist...a very old man who believed that there were paths through the ages that were accessible and that time was a myth. I became his student and eventually, after I received my inheritance, a financial backer of his expeditions. The scientist believed that there were lines of energy that crossed each other in certain areas, and that those areas were portals into time. Some have come to call these Ley Lines, though I don't think many have grasped their significance. He made it his life's work to catalogue these places, but I've still no idea how he found them."

"You never asked the question?" I asked.

"I never had the chance," Westlake replied. "On one of our last trips, he made the acquaintance of an ancient medium who told him that she could see him walking in a past century. She directed us to an antique dealer, and it was there that we bought this chair. The dealer had no idea how old it was, or that it had a special power, but being crafty, he sensed my mentors' excitement. We paid a small fortune for that chair." He paused and drank some of his beer.

"So it's the chair that's magic?" I looked at it, thinking that while it looked very old, sturdy and a bit oversized, there was nothing special about it.

"It has no power of its own, but when placed near these power areas, it's somehow able to focus the energy. The medium had said that once the chair is placed, 'you must see it to be it.' At the time I didn't understand it, but the old man seemed to know how to proceed. We took the chair to an isolated spot that apparently was a crossing of Ley Lines, and placed it accordingly. My scientist mentor sat in the chair and seemed to meditate for a minute...and then he was gone. Like you were that day in the tree, I was stunned. And then, within moments he reappeared. He was sobbing and babbling and it took me a bit to calm him down. He kept saying, 'I shouldn't have gone there!'"

"What did you do?" I asked. I had a lot of questions.

"I opened his flask and poured some whiskey into his mouth, and he coughed and sputtered his way back to sanity. He wouldn't tell me where he went, but as he was a religious man, I have an idea."

"Wow!" It was all I could say, I was speechless.

Hannah bumped him with her shoulder to get him to continue...It was then, in spite of all of our years together, that I first realized they were a couple. In the midst of my wide eyed wonder at everything I was being told, that realization made me very happy.

"I pestered him about how he did whatever he did, to the point of saying I would remove his funding, but still he resisted. Then he got ill, and though that flu would have barely hindered a younger man, it left his old body at death's door. He became very agitated in his last few days and demanded that I seek information about something called the Akashic Record. He then told me a phrase that he made me repeat, and also gave me what he said was a 'mental key' to unlocking the chair....and then he died."

I stared at him, in some part wanting to believe this entire story was made up for my benefit, but knowing it wasn't. Alex and John had long since left the area, but I was oblivious as to when.

"I quickly learned that the Akashic Record was something that mystics and seers had apparent access to; and it was how they made their predictions. Think of it as an enormous band of information, past, present, and future. My mentor took the next leap."

"I know what the phrase was," I said, interrupting.

Westlake looked at me and shook his head. "Of course you do."

"The medium said, 'you must see it to be it.' That's it right?" I was on board with it all.

"Yes that's the phrase," he said, "and if that's all it took to solve the mystery, I could have saved some years. But as it turned out, I needed to learn meditation, and history, and more about myself. Then one day I felt I was ready, and with some tricks my mentor had taught me, and the phrase you just said, I entered the Record. I found the day I wanted, used the mental key he gave me, and there I was, in the past."

"Where did you go?" I thought of all the possibilities available to a man who could go anywhere.

"I went to a day I remembered from a few years before, when I saw someone that made an indelible mark on my memory. I went back to see Hannah. That was a few years ago" he said with a smile.

"Then you're...how old?"

"In real years I'm twenty-eight," he replied, "but I've been out of this time period countless times. So has Hanna, so if you added our time away to our present ages, we're probably both in our mid- thirties."

Although he said it casually, I felt like I might vomit.

Hanna said, "Breathe Mike, breathe." Westlake gave me a moment, and then said this:

"I don't want your head to spin too much, and I think you know enough now to pick a destination. As I said before, stay away from violent places...and perhaps you'll enjoy it more if you can understand what people are saying. I do, however, have a vast array of clothing from different periods of history, so if you decided to visit, let's say, Paris in the seventeenth century, I'm sure we can find something to fit. If we do go to a place where you don't speak the language, I would simply ask that you let me do the talking."

"We...you said we, "I stammered. "So I won't be alone?"

"Heavens no!" he laughed and said with a smile towards Hannah, "we certainly can't have him running around through time on his own. How would he ever get back?"

They both laughed. For reasons I can't explain, perhaps their casual manner, I began to relax and in spite the fantastic story I'd just heard, I smiled and said to them both, "thank you."

"You're welcome," he said. "Now do I take that to mean you've decided to travel?"

"Has anyone ever refused?" I think I was buying time, but I'd already made my decision.

"Yes, as a matter of fact, Alex has." He looked towards Alex, who'd rejoined us with John, and smiled.

"It's just not for me," said Alex, who then turned to John and said, "John's gone on a few." John nodded, as if agreeing that he'd seen a certain movie.

"Yes, John has accompanied me on certain trips," said Westlake. "I find it comforting to have a friend along. In a way it anchors me. Now Mike, what'll it be?" He said that as casually as if I'd pulled in to a drive up to order a hamburger.

Now I know that when I tell you what choice I made, you'll think me a shallow nitwit. "You had all of history to choose, and you chose that!?" In my defense, I was nervous about getting too far out of my element, or too far away in time.

Westlake had an eyebrow raised at me and said, "Hmmm?"

"I want to see the Beatles, the first time they were on the Ed Sullivan Show. I want to be in the theater," is what I said. And even after all these years, I still don't regret it.

5

A Really Big Show

"How old would you be if you didn't know how old you were?"
Satchel Paige

"You can only be young once, but you can be immature forever."
Germaine Greer

Westlake looked at me for a moment, as if surprised, and then said, "That's a fantastic idea, for so many reasons! Now give me a few minutes to get some things together, and then we'll be off."

He moved quickly into the house, a man on a mission.

Hannah stared at me with a look of concern. "Are you ok?"

I thought about it, and in spite of every crazy thing they'd told me in the last hour, I trusted these people.

"I'm pretty excited," I said. "It looks like I'm going to see the Beatles."

Westlake returned carrying a few things and was quite animated as he placed them on the table in front of me.

"So, the date is February 9, 1964 and the location is the CBS Theater in New York. In the years to come many people will claim to have been there that night, but in truth, there were only seven hundred and twenty eight tickets chosen from over fifty-thousand mailed in requests," he said knowingly. "An estimated seventy-three million people watched it on TV. In some ways this event changed things for ever after."

I nearly asked how he knew that last bit, but I guess the answer was obvious.

"Now, as to your clothing; tuck your shirt in, and here's a clip on tie. Over that you're going to wear this crew neck sweater. I know only three years have passed, but this was a popular look in 1964. And your hair is too long. Hannah, would you please cut it back a bit with the scissors I brought out...and use this hair gel and part his hair on the side."

She put a towel around my neck and started cutting my hair. Oddly, this was the only problem I had with the travel preparation as I was nearly out of school and had been letting it grow.

"Don't worry Mike," Westlake said. "Hannah has cut my hair a number of times."

"You'll be just as handsome when I'm done," she added. I imagined her winking at me as she continued to snip.

"The important thing is to fit in. No one in the theater that night had a Beatle haircut, just the four boys on stage," Westlake said.

Within a few minutes Hannah had me meeting Westlake's specifications. She brushed the hair off my collar and the millionaire looked me over and nodded.

"There, now you look like some lucky kid from Idaho visiting his New York uncle," he said.

I sighed deeply, thinking what a dork I must look like. Then I said, "I guess I'm ready."

"Yeah, you are," he said," and here are your final marching orders. You'll stay at my side the whole time we're there, and you'll talk to no one unless they talk to you. Be vague, but really, no one is there to talk to you or me so just enjoy yourself."

"I can do that," I replied.

"Good. Now, go sit in the chair. I'll be standing behind it holding on to the back. When we get there, you'll be a little disoriented, but take a breath and it will pass quickly. They'll be so many hysterical teenagers there no one will look twice at someone trying to catch his breath."

I got up and slowly walked to the chair. This was really happening. I sat down and looked over at Hannah. I must have looked a little scared.

"It'll be alright, you're going to have a fantastic time and believe it or not, you'll be starving when you get back. I'll have some food ready," she said in a comforting tone.

Westlake stood behind the chair, patted me on the shoulder...

And then we were gone.

****

Everything turned black, the world spun once or twice and then I was bent over with my hands on my knees, looking down at a lushly red carpeted floor. Someone was patting me on the back and saying, "take a breath." I took a long breath and stood up to see Westlake, with a few sparkles around him, smiling at me.

"I know, I'm a little sparkly, I meant to tell you about that. I've never figured out why that is, but don't worry, it's only how time travelers see each other. Not a bad way to locate each other in case we get separated, eh?"

I was only half listening. We were standing in an alcove off to the side of the theater about three rows from the stage in the midst of people finding their seats and talking excitedly. Looking around the theater, the balcony seemed close enough to touch. To my immediate surprise I noticed a few sparkling people in balcony. More time travelers I wondered?

There were lots of adults, but many people my age, and I had to grudgingly admit that Westlake had dressed me right. By my current standards, there were very few cool looking kids in this theater...the Beatles really had culturally changed things; giving more meaning to Westlake's statement earlier.

"I meant to give you this...and this," he said handing me a ticket and a yellow card with a number on it. "It'll still be a while before show time, so let's go say hi."

I followed him in a semi daze to the right side of the stage, and when he held up his yellow card to a man guarding the door there, I held up mine. We passed through, walked up a few stairs and found ourselves backstage. There were lots of people moving around, some quickly, and I felt immediately that we were in the way. I stepped aside to let some person pass and realized that I'd stepped back onto someone's foot. I turned around to see John Lennon standing there.

"Bwawah!" I said in total shock and jumped back.

"And bwawah to you, lad," he said, affecting a limp as if I'd hurt him. He was wearing his glasses and I knew it would be a year before he wore them onstage. My first impression was how relaxed he seemed before what I thought was the biggest show of his life. Westlake was immediately at my side.

"John, my name is Patrick and this is my nephew Mike. We are delighted to meet you."

There was some hand shaking, during which I mumbled something that probably sounded like 'awoogaba.' John was gracious, but said over his shoulder to Westlake as he walked away, "he speaks a funny language."

"That went well," Westlake said as the other three Beatles walked by, close enough to touch. To say it was surreal would be to understate it. In the midst of the back stage chaos, they seemed casual and, I guess the word would be, confident.

"I shook his hand, and talked to him," I stammered to Westlake.

"Yes you did shake his hand, but I'm not sure the noises you made classify as talking to him." he said.

He smiled and chuckled. "Let's go back out and find our seats, the show will be starting soon."

We headed for the stage door, and back to the now filled theater. We took our seats, and in a few minutes the show began.

"Ladies and gentlemen...the Beatles," Ed Sullivan said and who knew seven hundred plus people could be so loud. The band kicked into 'All My Lovin,' and the sound of many hundreds of screaming girls nearly drowned them out. They were obviously used to this as it didn't seem to faze them in the least, and I was amazed at how they totally owned the moment. The energy coming from the stage was amazing, something I'd never experienced in my young life.

Things quieted down a bit during the next tune, when Paul sang the ballad *Til There Was You*. As soon as he finished, Westlake nudged me and said, "Come on." We once again flashed our yellow cards and were soon backstage again, this time watching them from the wings as they played *She Loves You*. The sound was a bit better from here without the screaming girls and I bounced along to the tune until they finished, at which point they bowed to the audience in perfect unison. It was a stunning performance.

They then walked quickly backstage, with Paul yelling out to no one in particular, "Hello America!" They walked past us and when John saw me he said, "Ooga booga." They walked down a hall to their dressing room, and I heard George say, "I can't hear a fookin' thing."

"We should head back now," Westlake said, and I thought he meant back to our seats, so I turned to head toward the door, but he put a hand on my shoulder.

"What I mean is, we should head home."

"But they play three more songs at the end of the show." I was so excited that I was almost levitating.

"I know they do, but you're new to this, and our travels demand more from us than you realize. Step over here for a minute."

We walked over to a darkened part of the back stage area.

"Now the next few minutes are going to be interesting, but keep your wits about you," he said.

But before I could ask him what he meant, we were gone.

****

Once again things went black, the world spun a couple times, and I heard someone say "here he comes" and I was sitting in the chair, looking at Westlake standing in front of me. I heard a loud gasp, and I looked over his shoulder to see the face of a startled young boy in a tree.

6

Here and There

"Reality leaves a lot to the imagination."
John Lennon

"Those who do not re-write history are doomed to remember it the way it really was."
Mike Girard

Westlake bent down and whispered to me, "I wanted you to see that, now let's get you home."

Again the world went black and it spun about...then there we were, back to where I instinctively knew we'd started earlier that day. Westlake was beaming at me as if I'd just told him the funniest joke. I looked over his shoulder...there was no small boy in a tree.

"Ok, you're disoriented, you're exhausted, and you're about as hungry as you can ever remember being. Try to relax and I'll answer your questions while we eat," he said.

I followed him to the picnic table where Hannah had spread out a feast of sandwiches, potato salad and soft drinks. I attacked the food like a starving dog despite having a million questions.

Hannah was sitting across from me. "Eat as much as you'd like."

She handed me a napkin, and as I wiped my mouth I realized tears were coming down my face.

"I saw the Beatles and I talked to John," I said as I ravenously ate anything within reach.

"Yes you did," Hannah said and she reached across to touch my hand. That simple thing made me take a breath.

Westlake let me eat, and waited. At some point when he thought I was ready he began to speak.

"You did so well, better than me my first time."

"Really?" I asked with a mouthful of food.

"Absolutely. Ok, let's start with the basics. As you probably now know, that type of travel uses a huge amount of your energy. I don't know why that is, but I made the mistake, once early on in my adventures, of staying at a place too long."

"Where was that?" I asked.

"That's unimportant and it was only for about a week, but when I returned I could barely walk. I was nearly feeble for days after. That's why we left before the show was over. I certainly didn't want your parents to question too much about your time here with us. As it is, your Dad thinks I'm tutoring you in history, which is pretty much true. "

He paused, while I continued eating. I had many questions, but at the moment, food was all I could think of.

"Another thing I learned early on is that we can't change the past. For those who would go back and mistakenly kill their great grandfather, or for those who would try and keep JFK from being assassinated...you could think you've done those things when you're back there, but when you return you realize that none of your actions had any affect. We could have prevented John from taking the stage, or we could have called in a fire alarm and caused the show itself to be cancelled. That's how it would seem to us while we there, but when we return we'd find out that nothing about that night had changed."

"How can that be?" I asked.

"Perhaps when we act too heavy handedly, we blink into some alternative time line that our actions caused. And maybe there are an unlimited number of time lines. All I know is that we change nothing in our own time line. That's why I like to try and only observe and not interfere. That way we get an unaffected view of the event we traveled to see."

By now I had eaten all I could hold, but weirdly, my eyes had not stopped leaking. I had just had the most amazing experience of my life, but I felt a great sadness that I was having trouble coming to grips with.

Westlake seemed to instinctively know what was going on with me. "Time for you to talk," he said.

"I had the best time," I said as my voice cracked. For a supposedly happy guy, I didn't sound or look like it. I gulped my emotions back. "It felt so real, and I know it was real...but now I feel like...I don't know, like they were so innocent and we're there watching them. They don't know what's going to happen, but we do."

My face was wet and I was breathing hard. I looked across at Hannah to see that she too had tears rolling down her cheeks.

Westlake's eyes seemed huge. He took a deep breath and explained. "Now we've come to the most important part of it all. No matter what we watch them do, they are sacred in their 'innocence' as you call it. They don't know we're there from another time and they don't know what they will become. Their place in the past is unchangeable. That's where your sadness comes from...mine too and it's why I showed you yourself in the tree. Now you'll know how sacred you were then, and hopefully how sacred you are now."

I was embarrassed that my tears still flowed, but I had no more questions, except one. "How can you still do it?"

"I'm a historian," he said. "I trade my feelings for a glimpse of what really happened. But it never gets easier, even after all this time. Now you've had a full day, and it's time you head home and hear your dad's good news. Are you ok to do that?"

I said I was and slowly nodded. Part of me never wanted this day to end, but I knew it had to.

The last thing Westlake said to me was this. "Good, because I have to go talk to a kid who is practically falling out of a tree. Good luck Mike and safe travels."

****

I said a short goodbye to them both, giving Westlake a firm handshake and Hannah a hug. I then went home to talk to my family about another mundane day of counting trees.

My Dad told the family the great news that he'd been offered the position of property manager by his 'friend' Pat. We were all happy for him, but my Mom, knowing it was a dream come true, was in tears while she hugged him.

"He and Hanna will be out of there soon," Dad said. He explained that they were going to be traveling extensively, and that it could be a year or longer before they returned.

"I asked him about hiring you to help me with running it, but he's convinced I can handle it myself. He told me that you had more important things to do. Do you know what he meant?"

"I think so, but it's hard to explain," I replied.

Dad just nodded and went back to talking about his plans to develop Westlake's property into a working farm. I was glad he didn't ask me to explain it because I wasn't sure I could at that moment.

I awoke the next morning with a feeling like I forgot something so I headed back through the woods, and up to the mansion. I walked up to the fountain and saw Alex standing there. Before I could talk he said, "They're gone, and they want you to know that they're not coming back anytime soon. They said you'll know what to do."

I knew they wanted me to travel, but I had no clue as to where or how. What I really wanted to do was start a band, but I was so crippled by my stage fright that I could see no way through to it. I was going to have to make some big decisions about most things going on in my life, but not today. Today I would finish a job I'd started years before. Even if no one cared about them, I still had a few barberries to count.

So that's what I did.

7

Purple Haze

"And if the band you're in starts playing different tunes, I'll see you on the dark side of the moon."
Pink Floyd

"The earth is a farm, we are someone else's property."
Charles Fort

"Blarga foo goba," the horrible black clothed creature said, as it stuck its giant lobster claw hand down in front of my face. It reminded me of one of the creatures from an old fifties horror movie I'd grown up watching at the drive-in.

I had just left North Station in Boston on a train headed for (I hoped) my hometown of Ipswich. It was a miracle I'd gotten this far, only now to have to deal with this vile creation from some nightmare world. I had money clutched in my hand that the abomination seemed to want. The woman sitting next to me didn't seem at all phased by the monster.

She leaned in close to me and said slowly and carefully, "he wants to know where you're going."

I looked from her up to the hideous thing and said, "Home." In response, and apparently agitated, it waved its lobster claw around in front of my face and made some raspy gurgling sounds.

"He wants to know where is home," said the woman, somehow able to translate the nonsensical sounds of the repulsive beast.

"Ipswich, Massachusetts," I said, as clearly as possible, lest the grotesque thing try and drag me into another dimension.

Then a funny thing happened, I looked up and saw the very puzzled face of the train conductor, a man dressed in black, and still holding his hand out in front of me. I passed him the money, he gave me my ticket, and with a still puzzled face he moved on.

I took a deep breath and wondered how much longer this was going to continue. It was late on a Saturday afternoon, and I was still tripping. Earlier that day I had taken, on the solid advice of a total stranger, something called Purple Haze. I don't think these were the kind of trips Westlake had in mind.

"It's really good acid, man," he said as he put the small pill in my hand and handed me a water canteen to wash it down.

The year was 1968, and I was in the first few months of what would be a year of living in Boston. It was also almost a year away from music, but given that I used to throw up before every show, I didn't feel it to be that much of a loss. I did feel some guilt though at not really following Westlake's suggestion to travel, but at least I was seeing some of the world outside of Ipswich.

It had been a beautiful day, and there was a summer series of free music events happening on Boston Common.

Concerts on the Common that day had featured Van Morrison, who I had heard of, and The Front Page Review, whom I hadn't. I'd been a fan of Morrison ever since he'd done a tune called *Gloria* with an Irish R&B band called Them back in 64'. It's hard to imagine this now, but there was no stage security, or even back stage area so when Morrison finished, and walked off the stage, I walked up and told him what a great fucking show it was.

"Thanks, man," he said and went on his way to do whatever rock stars of the day did after performing. I had ideas.

The opening band, The Front Page Review, had played a short set of mostly original catchy pop tunes. I would meet their lead guitar player later that fall and we'd become lifelong friends. That guy's name was Rich Bartlett, lead guitar player to this day of the Fools.

The drug had started to take affect about halfway thru Morrison's set, and my first reaction was how electric and alive everyone seemed. The stage wasn't very high, so I went back away through the crowd and decided to climb a tree for a better view.

"G--L--O--R--I--A, Gloria," Van sang, and I imagined the letters coming out of his mouth. Then...there were letters coming out of his mouth. Wow! Did I really have the power to imagine things and make them happen? I looked down from the tree at a pretty woman and imagined her naked. She stayed clothed. Unfortunately, my magic powers did not appear to extend beyond letters.

Then I heard a loud voice below me say, "Hey! Get the hell out of the tree!" It was the voice of a large scowling police officer. I'm one of those who's always had a pretty decent relationship with the police. I tend to do what they say, and treat them with respect. I would respectfully use a polite bit of reason on this one.

"I'm watching Van Morrison," I said. "I couldn't see him very well from in front of the stage." That sounded to me like a reasonable comment; being both factual and informative, and delivered with as much respect as my drug addled mind could summon up.

"I don't care if you're watching Humphrey Fucking Bogart! Get the fuck out of the tree!"

I was about to tell him that Humphrey Fucking Bogart was an actor not a singer, but I was distracted by the large colored letters coming out of his mouth. "Wow," I said.

"I'll give you fucking wow if you make me climb that tree to get you down," he said, his face was coloring. It had taken help from a stranger to get me boosted up the tree, so I couldn't imagine the policeman getting up the tree without the same kind of boost. The standoff ended when he got a radio call asking him to deal with some other apparently more important issue. His last words to me before he stalked off were, "if you're here when I get back, I'm taking you in."

I wondered if he would bring a couple officers along to boost him up the tree, or worse yet, bring a chainsaw and cut the tree down. In any event, it was probably time to climb down. There was only one problem: though I knew for a fact that I was only up about ten feet off the ground, the distance to earth now seemed much farther. I felt as if I, so far above the crowd, was in an upper stratosphere. Ah, the loneliness of the deep space astronaut.

While I was contemplating my re-entry into Earth's atmosphere, I was surveying the large crowd. To my surprise, I noticed a sparkle happening on the far side of the crowd, above and around two people. It was the kind of sparkle that only a time traveler can spot in another. Since I wasn't time traveling at the moment, I can only guess that the LSD was somehow heightening my perception. I was too far away to see them clearly, but the thought that it might be Westlake and Hannah sent me scrambling down the tree.

I made my way to the sparkling man and woman, and saw to my disappointment that they weren't my friends. When I look back on it now, they looked like a cartoon version of someone's idea of hippies...a Sonny and Cher kind of thing. This would be the proper party store buy for two travelers from the future going back to see Van Morrison on Boston Common in 1968. It wasn't unusual in those times, especially in concert venues, to have some stoned out nut walk up to you and say something odd. I was that stoned out nut.

"Wow, you guys aren't from around here, are you?"

I was smiling stupidly because I suspected their secret. Cher looked nonplussed but Sonny was kind of freaked.

"What are you talking about man?" he asked, looking nervous. I saw no words coming from his mouth.

"Sonny and Cher, ha!" I exclaimed with a laugh, at which point Cher's head snapped around towards me. She smiled and said, "Be cool, man."

Our eyes locked and I mellowed and nodded my head. She smiled at me and I smiled back. The man also nodded and smiled. They both knew that I shared their secret; they were time travelers. It was also the first time that it had occurred to me that besides Westlake, there were others who had unlocked the secret to traversing through time. I looked at Van onstage and remembered Westlake's dictum about staying anywhere too long and turned to tell them to be careful...but they were gone.

I walked to the stage, told Van how great he was, and headed for North Station to catch the train to Ipswich. The odd thing about this decision was that I had an apartment about a half a mile from the Common on Beacon Hill. Such is the frying egg of a brain on drugs that I decided that I needed to get to Cranes Beach, the locally iconic seven mile beach along the Ipswich shore. And, after encountering monsters on a train, I did.

I got off the train in Ipswich, rattled, but sure of my goal. I was lucky enough to flag down a high school chum that I hadn't seen for a while, who agreed to give me a ride to the beach. The chum said this before dropping me off:

"Jeezus, what's the fucking deal with your hair, you look like Louis the 14th!"

It was near dark when he dropped me off. My tunnel vision thought, for the last few hours, was simply that I had to get to the ocean, so it was with a purpose that I headed the last few hundred yards to the water.

Not far from the water, I saw some people sitting around a campfire. Back then it could happen at Cranes beach. I wandered over and was handed a beer by one of them, and a burnt hot dog on a stick by another of them. I realized that I hadn't eaten since the morning, so the meal seemed like a feast. The Purple Haze had finally worn off, and as I sat around the fire with about ten other very hairy people, I began to feel a great peace. It turned out that I was the only Ipswich native in the crowd. There were people from as near as Boston, and as far away as Seattle. It was a beautiful starlit night and the talk wandered into subjects like life after death, ESP, the Abominable Snowman, and flying saucers.

It seemed that we were all believers in ESP, but divided on the other subjects. I was telling the group about my own experience, an extended saucer viewing that had happened to my brother John and I a few years earlier, when Jay, the guy from Seattle, stood up quickly and pointed to the sky.

"What's that?" he asked. The sky to the north was rippling with color.

"That's the Northern Lights," I said, ever the smarty pants. I'd seen a display like this before but over the course of the next hour the rainbow colored ripples had spread to cover more than half the sky. By midnight the entire sky was glowing, and I was no longer confident of my analysis.

Given that none of us had ever seen anything like this, the more hysterical of us jumped to possible explanations.

"It could be that a nuclear war has started on the other side of the planet, and we're only now starting to see the atmospheric affects," I said.

Someone passed me a joint...if the world was ending, at least I would not face it sober and alone.

In another hour the lights began to fade. I learned the next day from the news that it was one of the more elaborate displays of Northern Lights ever witnessed. Soon the group began to disperse and head for the parking lot, leaving me to consider my options.

I could ask for a ride to my parent's house a few miles away, but showing up at two in the morning unannounced seemed like a bad idea. I thought vaguely of crashing in on Westlake and Hannah, but at last report, my Dad said they were still away.   Choice number three was to get a ride back to Boston, but the two heading there were going nowhere near Beacon Hill. The last choice was to spend the night on the beach. It really would have been much easier if the world had ended.

"What's your plan, man?" Jay's girlfriend Maryanne asked. They were the people I'd talked to the most.

"I guess I'm gonna spend the night here," I said.

"So are we," she replied. "We've got an extra sleeping bag if you need one."

Shortly we were in sleeping bags around the fire. I learned that Jay was a successful Seattle weed dealer, and that this trip, and the small camper they traveled in, were funded by that. Around sunrise, just before the tourists hit the beach, we all skinny dipped and then cooked some breakfast on the campfire. By 8:00 we were in their camper headed for my parents' house. The last thing Jay did, before they dropped me off, was to hand me a phone number.

"If you ever get to Seattle, call this number," he said. "It's my older brother. He'll always know how to get a hold of me."

With a wave, they drove off...two drifters, off to see the world, there's such a lot of world to see. I too would eventually see a lot of it, by benefit of my right thumb...and a certain very old chair.

8

The Road to...

*"At the end of the day, your feet should be dirty,
your hair a mess, and your eyes sparkling."*
Shanti

"So what I don't get" I said to Bhangura, "is why you
shave your head, and what's with that little bit of hair in
the back?"

We'd just met a few hours before in the parking lot
of a roadside restaurant just off I-5, an interstate that
goes from California to Washington. I was in the final
leg of hitch hiking across America. For the last year I'd
finally been taking Westlake's advice about getting away
from Ipswich. There was involvement in a band of two
whenever I was back home, but I was still the terrified
stick figure on stage.

On this trip it had taken me three weeks and many
adventures to get this far, and if I continued to get good
rides, I would soon be at my destination, Seattle. My
goal was to find my beach friends, Jay and Marianne.
How crazy is it that, before cell phones, and after only a
one time meeting, I was off to find these people? But
back then it seemed that the highways were crowded
with hitch hikers.

Bhangura saw my hand made sign, made with a
marker on a piece of cardboard that said SEATTLE. He

was going there too, so there we were together, me with long King Louis the 14th curly hair and him, a Krishna devotee, bald with a topknot, reminiscent of no one I

had ever met.

We'd gotten picked up by an older hippy driving a van who had some weed. I was well into weed by this point, but of course my new friend declined. Bhangura was an earnest young kid, still a bit nervous about the path he had chosen, but not me...I was a devout stoned dumbass. It was why I, as a young nitwit, would ask such a blunt question to someone I just met about a religion I knew nothing about.

"The topknot is called a *shikha*, it's a way for God to pull me out of the water of life and into the eternal."

I just stared at him because I had no answer to that, and maybe I still don't, but not long after I asked him that, we got dropped off at an interstate roadside restaurant, just over the line into Washington State.

The thing about Washington State was this; hitch hiking was illegal. I knew this from encounters with other hitchers I'd met on the west coast. I'd heard though of a way to possibly get around it; I would hold my Seattle sign, not on the highway, but on the entry ramp to the highway. I forget whether Bhangura agreed to this logic, or just came along, but within a short period of time, we were both arrested.

"Get in the car boys," the arresting officer said; a very large man with a big belly and smoky the bear hat. I protested and said we weren't hitching, as there was no thumb involved. He said we were soliciting a ride, which was also illegal in Washington.

"Get in the car, boys," he repeated, a little more sternly than the first time. We did as he ordered. So much for what you hear from other hitchers.

He took down our names, having a little trouble with Bhangura, whom he decided to call Bingo. Soon enough we arrived at King County Jail, and for the first and only time in my life, I was incarcerated. The good news was, we'd finally made it to Seattle, the bad news was...well, we weren't going to be seeing it for a while.

The cop who'd nabbed us pulled to a stop in front of the jail, got us out of the car and for the first time, handcuffed us.

"Protocol," he said.

Then he brought us in to be processed. Our possessions were taken, we were finger printed, and brought inside where we were told to shower and given orange jump suits. I was quick to learn that the King County jail was no small time affair; it had a couple hundred prisoners, some doing extended time for things like murder and armed robbery. What better place to put two hard cases like us; Louis the 14th and Mahatma Gandhi?

****

"If you don't shut the fuck up," yelled Frank at the drunk man on the bunk across the room, "I'm gonna come over there and hurt you."

Frank wasn't kidding, and the drunk grumbled and closed his mouth. It was our first night in jail. We'd had the bad luck to get arrested on a Saturday and as the judge held weekly court days only on Friday, we were going to spend nearly a week in the slammer.

We were in a large cell with six bunk beds totaling twelve beds. Aside from Bhangura and me, there were three drunk and or homeless people and Frank. Frank was the only permanent resident. Each night the cops would deliver whomever they'd picked up off the streets as too drunk or rowdy and keep them overnight in this cell. Frank's unofficial job was to keep the drunks quiet and peaceful til morning, a job he took very seriously. In payment he would receive cigarettes from the guards and get to eat whatever food the hungover drunks refused to eat the next morning.

He was a big kid, about six foot four, with a crew cut and he looked like he could play linebacker in the NFL. I say kid, but at twenty-five, he was then five years older than me.

Earlier that day we'd heard two of the jailers gripe about how crowded the cells were, and wonder, "Where can we put these two freaks?"

The other guard said, "We'll put them in with Frank," and then finished it with a loud, "ha!"

The guard then put us in the cell and said to Frank, "Say hi to your new bunkmates...this one's Mike and this one's Bingo."

Frank looked puzzled for a moment and then started to laugh, and continued laughing until he was nearly bent over and hanging onto a bunk. "We'll I'll be," he said, catching his breath, "if it isn't Jessie James and Doc Holiday."

I guess we didn't look too intimidating. Perhaps that's why he instantly seemed to adopt us. Frank also had a contrarian streak that we somehow spoke to.

"They put you in here because they think I'll beat you up. They don't know me," he said.

The three of us then talked for a few hours. We learned that Bhangura was from Chicago and that I was from Massachusetts, and that Frank was from Tacoma, Washington.

Frank had been in for three years on a charge of aggravated assault and he had eight months left. He seemed impressed that two weird looking kids had been able to travel so far on their own.

"Shit," he said, "it's only been a couple of years, but so much has changed since I've been in here. If I wasn't locked up I'd be out there like you guys, just fuckin' seeing the world."

So it was that on that first night, when the drunks came in, and one of them looked at Bhangura and me and said, "what kind of freak show is this" that Frank threatened the man into silence. The next morning breakfast was served for six but as Frank had predicted, only the three of us were hungry.

Food was served twice daily in jail, at seven a.m. and at four p.m., and the rest of the time was god awful boring. To pass the time, we told stories; they learned about Ipswich clams and houses built in 1640 that were still standing. I learned about the perfect type of land for growing grapes, as Frank's dream was to become a winemaker. Frank and I learned about the God Krishna, and watched in silence as Bhangura would pray, sometimes for hours, eyes closed and head bobbing.

There was an empty paper bag and four checkers in the room, so Frank and I played a game that involved putting the bag in one corner and trying to throw checkers in it from the opposite corner. We would bet an apple or a sausage on the outcome, and it got quite spirited, but mostly it just passed the time.

On the afternoon of the third day, there was a loud buzzer that went throughout the jail, and Frank said, "The preacher is here." With that, all the steel cell doors slid open to be replaced by the classic bars that most people picture when they think of a jail. Now I saw that about twenty cells faced a large common square area, in which had been placed a small podium. Behind that podium was a round, bald man wearing a black robe. In a loud voice and in the droning but dramatic manner of most southern Baptist men of the cloth, he began to preach to us.

"And the Lord said blah blah blah etc." You know the routine; telling us that though we were thieves, liars, and fornicators, there was still a place in God's kingdom for us if only we would repent. The reactions of the prisoners were varied. Some dropped to their knees the moment the doors slid aside. Others yelled 'amen' or 'hallelujah' which seemed to make the preacher get even more wound up. It was after the word 'fornicators' that pretty much all of the prisoners cheered and hooted, fornicators one and all. At some point the preacher finished and began making the rounds to stand for a few minutes in front of each cell and talk quietly with the inmates.

By the time he got to our cell, Frank had long since gone back to lie on his bunk. That left Bhangura and I to talk to the preacher. He looked at his list and asked, "Which one of you is Bingo?"

"Neither of us," I said. He looked a little confused and then said, "Which one of you is Mike?"

"That would be me," I said.

"Now Mike," he said, giving me a concerned fatherly look, "what brought you to this place?"

"A police car," I said.

I could hear Frank snort loudly behind me.

"No," the preacher said, trying again. "What was the nature of the crime that has brought you to this house of detention?"

"Hitch-hiking," I said.

"What?" he looked over his shoulder at a stoned faced guard to see if I was either a plant, or a simpleton. He looked back at me.

"Hitch-hiking," I repeated.

"Hard core fucking hitch-hiker," Frank yelled to no one in particular.

The preacher sighed in disappointment, and turned to move on to the next cell, and maybe more fertile ground...obviously he'd been hoping to talk to another rapist or murderer. Before he left he looked at me grumpily and said, "Get a haircut, and you," motioning to Bhangura, "grow some hair."

I turned to see Frank giving me a wry look. "A police car," he said. "Ha!"

Later that night and out of the blue, with no prompting, Frank told his story.

"My Dad is a trans con truck driver so he was away a lot. I came home early from work one day and found his brother, my uncle, fucking my mom. It was consensual. I told him to get dressed and get the fuck out. I waited for him outside, and when he tried to push his way past me, I knocked him down. He's a big guy and he got up ready to have at it with me so I beat him up."

"Holy crap," I said softly.

"My mom called the cops and when they came, he said I attacked him. I wasn't gonna claim any different until my mom agreed. When I took another swing at him, one of the cops hit me with his stick across the back of my knee. I was still pretty hot and I knocked him down. I stopped when the other cop took his gun out. If I hadn't hit the cop, I might have got probation. Anyhow, that's what brought me to this house of detention. That, and a police car," he said with an eyebrow towards me.

Though there were so many questions we could have asked him, Bhangura and I were silent and barely breathing. Frank looked at us both, stood up, and said, "Ok, we're playing for sausages, most checkers in the bag, two out of three times wins."

Our last morning in jail was a bit somber. Frank was grouchy, maybe because no drunks had shared our cell, or maybe because we were leaving, and Bingo and I were anxious about our impending release.

Bhangura never talked much; he nodded if he agreed, smiled at jokes, and looked thoughtful when someone talked. This morning after breakfast however, he walked to the head of the table and sang this loudly and in a pretty good voice to Frank:

"There was an inmate had a friend and Bingo was his name oh...B-I-N-G-O, B-I-N-G-O, B-I-N-G-O, Bingo was his name oh."

Bhangura then bowed and took a seat. We all laughed and then Bhangura reminded Frank that if he prayed to Krishna, his remaining eight months would go by much quicker. Frank gave us the curious head shake and said, "They'll be taking you out pretty soon."

And shortly after, they did, and with a look back at a friend, Bingo and I were walked down a corridor and marched into court. The judge decided that we had paid our debt to society, and soon Bingo and I were having an uncomfortable moment in front of the jail. We talked for a bit, I gave him a wave, and he gave me a hands folded prayer nod, and that was it.

We meet odd and fascinating people in sometimes stressful situations. I never saw either one of them again, but I hope Bingo found his god and Frank found his vineyard.

They were my friends.

9

Some Like it Wet

Question: When is it summer in Seattle?
Answer: Last year it was on a Wednesday.

I'll be right up front about it; the six months I spent in Seattle was the longest year of my life. You'd think it would be my kind of city; it's young, pretty hip, and has an energetic music scene. The state of Washington itself is as quirky and odd as any place in America. It also leads the country in the most Bigfoot sightings. It was also here on June 24, 1947, that small plane pilot Kenneth Arnold saw something in the sky not far from him; nine discs that he said were "saucer shaped." The press coined the term 'flying saucers' and the modern age of UFO chronicling had begun.

And in terms of home grown celebrities, Washington State has many, including two of my all-time faves; Jimi Hendrix and Bruce Lee (yeah, yeah, I know Bruce was originally from Hong Kong but he settled in Seattle). So with all of this going for it, why do I list it as my least favorite place in America? I'll give it to you in one word---rain.

It pretty much starts raining as soon as you cross the border. The foliage is as thick and green as any place on the planet and the reason is rain. Seattle itself has become well known for the abuse of two drugs...coffee and heroin. People over using the former are fighting the rain, and people using the latter are surrendering to it.

Time has probably colored my memory, but I think it rained at least some part of every day I was there. I was told that summers were relatively dry and sunny, but I showed up near the end of October, just in time for the rainy season. According to the National Weather Service, it rains on an average of one hundred and fifty-seven days a year, most of that happening between October and March. That would mean it rains for one hundred and fifty-seven days out of a possible one hundred and eighty. That's pretty damn wet.

Jay had told me that if I ever got to Seattle to call his brother, so after I got out of jail, I did. His brother then connected me with Jay.

Jay was thrilled to hear from me and it wasn't long before he and Marianne came and picked me up. We drove through a steady rain until we arrived at their house; a cute three bedroom split level ranch on a fenced quarter acre lot. The streets in the neighborhood were all tree lined and the houses were pretty close together. As we got out of the car and made our way through the puddles of rain to their front door, I heard someone from the other side of the fence say, "oh boy, more hippies."

"That's my neighbor," Jay said. "He's kind of an asshole." We went inside where I was immediately made to feel at home. As I told them of my hitch hiking adventures I realized that Jay and Marianne were still the same friendly people I'd met back on the beach in

Ipswich. Jay's weed dealing business was still going well, and Marianne had recently entered nursing school.

The only down side to my living with them was Marianne's cooking. Since I'd last seen them, they had become vegetarians, and though her goal was to give the tofu, lentils, and rice something resembling flavor, it was a goal rarely achieved. There were more than a few uncomfortable meals around the kitchen table.

"It's all natural," Jay would say, as he struggled to get down another bite of whatever concoction was on the table.

So is dirt I thought. After that first day with them, I walked down to a local burger stand through the pouring rain and gorged myself on the evil meat.

Jay asked me what I had in mind for work. It was something I hadn't really thought of...ah youth! He suggested that I join him in his life of crime. He was no longer street dealing. His business has progressed to the point where he was dealing many kilos to regional suppliers.

His thinking was that he would front me a kilo, which I would break into ounces, or 'lids' as we called them. After I sold them, I would give him half the money and keep the rest. He suggested that I go to that very same burger stand, which was across the street from a large factory, and hang about around lunch time. Back when he was street dealing it was one of his more lucrative stops. The idea of daily visiting a burger stand had instant appeal to me, so I agreed to his proposal.

(Can we now have a moment to deal with all of you 'oh my god, he was a drug dealer' people? I sold no hard drugs. If it makes you feel better, don't think of me as a drug dealer, think of me as someone with a more romantic occupation...a bootlegger perhaps; except that instead of booze, I sold weed to adults. Let's face it, as far as our current laws are changing, I was way ahead of my time.)

Time, you say? Jeezus, Mike isn't it time you get Westlake back into the story!? You introduce us to a fascinating character and then he disappears. What the flying fuck?

To which I respond: first of all, you know I don't like it when you use that kind of language. Second of all, I'm trying to tell the story mostly in the order that it happened. Westlake and Hannah will return. All things in good...um...never mind. Now let me get back to my story.

The next day Jay and I drove, through the heavy rain, for about forty-five minutes to a summer camp he owned deep in the woods north of Seattle. It was here that he kept his product. I should mention that Jay and Marianne never smoked at home, and that Jay kept no weed in the house. At the summer place, he had a padlocked storage room with large plastic containers stacked against one wall. He opened one and in it I saw three neatly wrapped packages, each package weighing two point two pounds, or in other words, a kilo.

He brought one into the main room, and after setting it on the picnic table, he took a small scale off the counter. Over the course of the next hour, we weighed and bagged the stuff in small plastic sandwich bags. We also smoked some, so that I would know what I was selling. Having said that, I could never tell when Jay was high, maybe he talked a little more, but that was the only indication. On the other hand, while I've always been able to hold my alcohol, I get stupidly high on weed. It's why I quit doing it years ago.

And now for a quick interjection entitled:

WHY MIKE DOESN'T SMOKE WEED

Pardon me if we quickly time travel to the current era and take a sudden detour. This story takes place just a couple of years ago. We Fools were hired to play what was termed a 'rock festival' in central Maine. It was a three day outdoor event featuring bands from all over the region and culminating with us playing on Sunday afternoon. The summer event would be staged at a ski resort, with the stage built at the bottom of the mountain making it a natural amphitheater.

On paper it looked like it was going to be something special. There was only one problem, but it was a big one; it seems that the promoter did nothing to promote the show. No TV, no radio, and no print ads were devised to alert the general public. So the general public stayed home...in droves.

(First of all, I'm taking it for granted that you know who the players in my band are. Though it's late in this game, here is your quick Fools' primer. On one guitar is my friend from five years old, Stacey Pedrick. On the other guitar is my friend from nineteen years old, Rich Bartlett. On drums is my friend since 1983, Leo Black. Finally, on bass is my new friend of eight years, Eric Adamson. These are my people, and it's not an exaggeration to say that I would trust them with my life.)

The first inkling that the rock festival was going south was a call from Stacey. He had arrived while Rich and I were in transit.

"There's nobody here, and I mean there is nobody here," he said. We pulled into the parking lot not long after and realized Stacey was not kidding. In a parking lot that could have held five hundred cars, with room for more on the field...there were about twenty. It was a stunningly bad turnout.

A word about shows like this; these kind of let downs can be soul crushing but one thing about being in a band that has existed since 1977 is that you've pretty much seen it all. Before a show I might have a beer, but my first thought at seeing the crowd of thirty people sitting in front of the stage was this: today I will drink. Rich and I walked around the site, found Stacey and the rest of the band, and met the terrified promoter. We also met the Russian born groundskeeper who invited Rich and I into his shed for vodka shots.

"To Fools," he shouted as we tossed them down.

It was about thirty minutes before the show and I was dressed like a priest when I met another groundskeeper. The priest outfit was so that I could marry the crowd, a bit I'd done many times over the years to start a show. The groundskeeper didn't know I was in the band. He may have thought I was a real priest but maybe not because he offered me a hit on a joint. It was my first hit in years. I remember laughing. I remember him giving me a joint. I remember smoking it. Then I sort of remember seeing a golf cart and stealing it. It's hazy but I remember driving up the mountain chased by an upset gardener.

"Hey!" he kept yelling as he chased the stoned priest up the hill. The priest however was apparently answering to a higher calling and only drove faster. The gardener was in good shape and just about to overtake the priest, when the cart swerved wildly to the left and headed back down the slope at a stupid speed.

"Ha!" yelled the priest triumphantly as the exhausted gardener paused to catch his breath. At about seventy-five yards from the stage, the band sees the priest hell bent for leather heading for the stage.

The band starts the first song, at the same time moving back from the front of the stage, out of harm's way in case the priest doesn't stop in time. At the last possible moment, the priest stomps the brake, jerks the wheel, and slides to a perfect stop directly in front of the stage. He exits the vehicle and crawls onto the stage but he is laughing too hard to talk or sing. When he finally composes himself, he realizes he has forgotten the words to a song he's sung a thousand times.

By now the angry and confused gardener has finally reached his golf cart. The priest looks down on him and makes the sign of the cross...and the pissed off gardener, confused by the religious reference, decides not to hurt the priest. And all of that happened before I sang a single note. It's why I don't smoke weed.

[Now back to Seattle.]

Jay and I finished up at his weed farm and drove back to his house with the thirty-five single ounce bags of pot. Do the math if you care. Because Jay was not only a good but careful business man, he led me to a place, through the rain, into his backyard. His back yard was a small high fenced area of well-kept lawn with a Madonna statue near the back fence. It had puzzled me because he was the least religious person that I knew. He moved the statue aside and I saw that the wide base of it disguised a kind of trap door area that hid a pit in the ground. It was here that I would place whatever unsold stash I had.

It was a pretty easy drug dealing, sorry, I meant bootlegging gig. I would show up at the burger joint around noon, buy a burger and hang out at the tables in the parking lot. Because it was always raining, the burger joint had erected covered areas and it was there that I plied my trade.

After a few days of asking questions like, "anybody got a joint," I realized that the place was ready for my business. Over the course of almost six months, I made more money than I'd ever seen before. The gig however was not without its drawbacks. Jay instructed me about how to keep a low profile. My name wasn't Mike, it was Bill or Jack, or whatever I thought it was on any given day. I would also dress differently and leave the place headed in different directions. I carried the stuff in a backpack and conducted my transactions in what I thought was a discrete manner. Despite all my precautions, there came a day when the shit hit the you know what...um...I guess that would be the fan.

I was plying my trade, as a bootlegger, and feeling pretty good about it. As much as I grew to despise Seattle weather, I liked the people I met...a lot. It's a weird biz selling illegal drugs to people. Though they want what you're selling, they often look at you as the low life they need to go through to get what they want. I was that low life, and though most of the nice people of Seattle didn't treat me that way, there was always a tinge of it.

Because I was a drug dealer, I mean bootlegger, it was assumed that I was tougher than I was, or that I was the happy face behind something more ominous. Both things were of course ridiculous. I'm not

physically imposing, nor threatening in any way, and
Jay was the least ominous person you would ever meet.
At times though, when someone said they would pay me
and didn't, I would affect a pose that suggested
consequences. They of course never happened but
thankfully the word never got out that I was clawless.

It was on another rainy day, late in March, while I
was awaiting the lunch time crush from the factory
across the street, that I felt a tap on my shoulder. I've
always prided myself on my ability to sense anyone near
me, so I was surprised.

"Hey," Patrick Westlake said, giving me an odd grin.
To say I was stunned would be an understatement.
Though he was however many years older than me, he
looked the same as I remembered him at our first
meeting, when I was eight. He knew I was
hyperventilating and allowed me to settle down before
he talked.

"So what the hell are you doing?" he asked, eyeing
me carefully. "I have no moral problem with what
you're doing, but was I wrong about you?"

"How'd you find me?" I asked, not wanting to
answer the other questions. It had been enough years
since I'd last seen him that I'd almost begun to question
his reality.

"It's not complicated. Your Dad told me you were
here and gave me your address. He and your Mom are
worried about you. You should call them, they miss you.
Oh and Hannah says hi."

The information was delivered so casually that it
almost put me at ease, but not quite.

The lunch crowd from across the street had started to arrive and I was feeling a disconnect that I couldn't come to grips with.

"I think I'm gonna be sick," I said and I wasn't lying. Westlake led me to a car and we got in. He drove away from the burger place and I didn't complain. At some point he pulled over at a roadside diner. We went in and found a booth. Even though I was still a little queasy, he ordered us a couple of BLTs. Once the food arrived he started talking.

"I'm not here for you, I'm here on other business but because you're also here, it's a coincidence I couldn't ignore. It's good to see you, Mike."

"It's good to see you too," I said. I was feeling better. "Are you here from the past?"

"No," he said. "I'm here in real time. Lately I've been spending a lot of time in the present. Now tell me what you've been up to the last few years."

Between bites of my sandwich, I started telling him about living in Boston, about singing in crappy cover bands, and still feeling terrified to do it, about hitch hiking, about spending a week in jail, and about my friends Jay and Marianne. The words were soon spilling out of me, the way they do when you're talking to an old friend you haven't seen in a while.

He listened carefully, the way he always did, asking questions about my time in Boston and laughing at my jail story. Once I was done catching him up, he said this:

"Well, you've lived a lot in the last few years. I told you to get out and see the world and you have. I'm sure you've learned some things that can only be learned by experience. I have to tell you though...you've chosen a very dangerous occupation. I watched you leave there yesterday and then I wandered in like a tourist and asked about where I might get some stuff. Your many names and clothing choices are amusing your customers. It's too small a burger joint to expect your daily arrivals not to raise some eyebrows, especially amongst the regulars."

I knew that everything he said was true, and I felt a strong paranoia building inside me.

"May I ask how much you've made in this endeavor?" He was never one to leave the facts off the table.

"I've got about seven thousand dollars," I said. It was huge amount back then for a novice bootlegger who'd only been legging his boots for six months.

"I feel you are in jeopardy. Do you want to bookend your stay in Seattle with another term behind bars? This time they won't fuck around with you. You'll be in there for a while and you'll have a permanent record. Real prison time is much different than the pre-trial jail they kept you in before."

He never swore. I was sold. It was time to leave.

We finished up our meals, and soon enough he was dropping me off at my place.

"One more thing Mike," he said. "When you get back to Ipswich and start playing music again, I'd like you to try a mental exercise. Just before you go onstage, I want you to imagine that you've just arrived there on a time jump."

"Why, "I asked.

"After our Beatles trip, what was the one thing that stuck in your mind about everyone you met in the past?"

I thought for a minute. "That they were kind of...sacred," I said.

"Exactly. So before you go onstage, I want you to try and believe that you've just arrived in that time period. Then go out and treat your audience, whether it's 50 people or 5,000, as if they are sacred. Will you try that for me? "

"Okay."

That exercise changed my life. Thank you Patrick.

We shook hands, and after dropping me home, he drove off into whatever mystic place he inhabited. I walked in preparing my 'I'm leaving' story for Jay and Marianne but instead of telling them that night, I went to bed. It was around midnight that I heard some loud noises coming from the house next door.

"Put your hands above your head," said a very loud police sounding voice from the house next to us. I knew some important shit was happening and I walked out onto the front lawn. Jay was already there looking over the fence at the chaos next door. It was quite a sight. There were three cruisers with lights all popping in that front yard. The hippy hating dude next door was standing in undershorts and tee shirt with his hands over his head.

"What the fuck is this about," he was yelling.

We found out the next day that our neighbor had been selling methamphetamines. It was a total shock, but it reminded me of the possible pitfalls I might see if I stuck around in my present occupation. While meth was and is a heinous drug, and weed isn't, the law back then wasn't making much of a discrimination. With all that in mind and my talk with Westlake...the next morning I said my goodbyes to a not so surprised Jay and Marianne.

"Get back to music," was the last thing Jay said.

And eventually, I did.

10

Back From Seattle

"From Ipswich, Massachusetts, entertainment capital of the world, and home of the fried clam, please welcome, The Fools!!"
Fred Mozdziez (Number 7) introducing the band

"The nice thing about living in a small town is that when you don't know what you're doing, someone else does."
Immanuel Kant

"But why can't I go with you?"

I was trying not to sound like I was whining, but even to my ears, I wasn't succeeding.

Westlake slowly shook his head and said "you're not ready."

I'd been back home in Ipswich for about a week. My trip back from Seattle was a five day affair. On a college cafeteria bulletin board, I'd seen a notice that three people in a van were looking for a fourth to share driving and gas expenses on a trip to Boston. I met up with them, we agreed on terms, and left that afternoon. Other than food or bathroom stops, we drove nonstop, each of us driving about six hours, while the others slept, talked or listened to the radio.

It was an uneventful trip, and I was thrilled to be home. It turned out to be good timing, as my parents were soon going to spend a couple months visiting relatives in Arizona, and were delighted that I would be able to housesit for them. It was my parents' first lengthy vacation in years, and my Dad made a point to tell me that Westlake had no issue with him being away.

"He said that when you get settled you should come up and see them," he added.

He then told me that 'Pat and Hannah' had recently been back spending more time in Ipswich, after being away for most of the last couple of years. My Dad talked about them as if they were old friends. My Mom said that Patrick had become a regular guest of Dad's at his VFW. That made me oddly happy.

I could have taken my car and driven through the front gate, and up the long hill, but maybe for old time's sake, I walked across the marsh and up through the woods. It had been a few years since I'd taken that walk, and it brought me back to my childhood, to the point where I had to resist a strong urge to climb my spying tree. Though I'd recently seen Westlake in Seattle, I hadn't seen Hannah since the day of my Beatles trip. I was a little nervous.

I found them in the last place I'd seen them together, having lunch at the picnic table near the fountain. I yelled out a 'hello' as I stepped out of the woods, so as not to startle them. Hannah looked up and saw me, and came running.

"Mike it's so good to see you," she said as she hugged me. Then she stepped back, looked me up and down, gave me an odd smile, and said, "You've grown up."

This caused me, the seasoned world traveler, to blush furiously, but thankfully Westlake ignored that and patted me on the back as we walked to the table.

"I'll go get us some more food," he said, and added with a smile to Hannah, "Mike can fill you in on his criminal exploits."

I must have looked a little moon faced but her words calmed me.

"It's ok," she said. "He told me all about it. And he's only being sarcastic because he was worried about you. I think he was feeling like some of your decisions were a result of him encouraging you to leave Ipswich and see the world. He considers you a friend, and for such an old soul, he has precious few."

I said what I thought. "I feel like I've disappointed you both."

"Oh please," she with a smile and an eye roll. "Patrick and I were nothing but trouble when we were your age. We're both just happy that you got out of Seattle in one piece."

With that, the ice was totally broken, and I was back talking at ease with a friend I hadn't seen in years. I told her about the preacher I'd seen in jail, and about Bingo and Frank. She laughed with me and yet understood the kismet, never see 'em again, personal gravity of the story.

"Does he still...travel," I finally asked her, as if it wasn't on the tip of my brain from the moment we'd sat down.

"Yes he does," Westlake said, suddenly reappearing with a plate load of food. He set the food in front of me and said, "Let's eat."

We did, but I couldn't wait till we finished.

"Can I come with you the next time you go somewhere?" I asked.

"Someday maybe, but for now, you're not ready," he said it so casually that I knew it was true.

"How do I get ready?" I asked.

He eyed me carefully, with a smile I never fully understood, and said, "I would need your total concentration. No drugs, no alcohol, no fried food, and no anything unless I say you can."

"I can do that," I replied.

"I'm not done yet," he said. "You would need to train your body and your mind, and there are no short cuts. This thing you want to do demands all of your being, otherwise, you will make me guilty of your death. I showed it to you years ago because I saw a light in you, but if I was wrong about what's available to you as a being, the guilt is on me. You are my friend, I don't want that burden hanging over my head."

I looked across at Hannah, and saw her awaiting my response. Westlake took another bite of his food, as if it were any other day. "Your thoughts?"

"Tell me how to do it," I said.

And so for the next 6 weeks, as per Westlake's instructions, I started running five miles, and then ten miles a day, to the point where I became in tune with my body. Since my parents were away, and I had no one to answer to at home, he and Hannah spent evenings teaching me, with meditation, how to control my busy mind. There were also hours spent in breath control, and enormous amounts of hydration.

It was the most intense experience of my life, and around the time that I felt like a gun ready to fire, Westlake came to me and simply told me we were good...and we were.

I was ready to once again travel into the past and of all the places to ever go, when you can go anywhere you want, he surprised me as to his choice. But then again, he's a historian.

11

Fixing a Hole

"Sometimes a deep canyon is just a deep canyon. But then there's the Grand Canyon, something visible from space. Now that's a canyon."
Altor Watt

"The Grand Canyon is 277 miles long: 28 miles wide at its widest, and 1 mile deep at its deepest."
Info from Grand Canyon brochure

"Is this real," I asked looking at an ancient newspaper I'd been handed and just read. It was an edition of the Arizona Gazette and dated April 5, 1909.

"The newspaper's real, but as to the story, that's what we're going to try and find out," Westlake said.

He and Hannah had kept quiet while I read the story, and both seemed to now be judging my reaction. It was an odd but fascinating article. It claimed that a man, G.E. Kincaid, a "hunter and explorer all his life," had discovered an enormous cave system in the far depths of the Grand Canyon. He was apparently coming down the Colorado River, looking for 'mineral' which probably meant gold, when he noticed a discoloration high up on a canyon wall. After much difficulty, he claimed to find a cave opening. He went on to say that many artifacts, of an apparent Egyptian or Tibetan nature had been discovered.

The article also claimed that he was now aided and joined by a professor, S.A. Jordan and that the search was funded by the 'Smithsonian Institute.' According to the account, the cave system contained mummies, hieroglyphics, and numerous other artifacts of apparent great age. And, according to the story, the fact that the cave entrance was a couple hundred feet above the current river level likely spoke to thousands of years of river erosion, and the great antiquity of the find. Whether or not the story was true, the article appeared to be genuine.

"But if it's true, why haven't we heard anything else about it?" It made no sense.

"That's the real question," Westlake answered, "because if it was simply a sensational bit of nonsense to boost readership, it would only have worked for that day's edition. But I haven't found any other evidence of that paper printing bogus stories. And if it was simply an April fool's joke, it was four days too late."

I laughed. "So we're going to the Grand Canyon to look for a cave that no one else has discovered since 1909?"

It seemed like the wildest of goose chases, but I didn't care; I was just excited at the prospect of once again traveling back in time. For all I cared, we could be visiting a rock in Utah, or a bug in California, but because we'd be going into the past to do it, I was all in.

"Actually, I've been to the canyon a few times, both present and past. The first time, I went back to the period and after some difficulty, and much investigation, I found evidence of a large caravan heading deep into the canyon. The trail ended at the river where they must have boarded their boats. But that took me days to find out, and as I physically over stayed my welcome, it took me more days to recover."

"He was a mess," Hannah added, giving Westlake a withering look that told me all I needed to know about how much his overstay and the effects of it had worried her. Time travel was hard; though you didn't feel it while you were at your destination, the demands on your body were extreme. It was why Westlake had been training me. Though at twenty I was already inherently quite active and fit, he and Hannah, for my own safety, had pushed me to the next place.

Westlake continued. "The next time I went in, I picked an earlier time and placed myself on a beach well down the river. I had the look of a prospector and set up camp. Towards the end of that day four good sized boats came down the river carrying about twenty men and supplies. I acted as if I needed help and ran to the river's edge yelling to them. I was hoping they would pick me up and take me with them. But a tall man in the front of the first boat said loudly to his company, 'keep going,' and they did, with hardly a look at me. It surprised me as it was not in keeping with the frontier standards of that time."

I pictured myself on that bank, in 1909, calling out to strangers from the past, not knowing whether or not I would be picked up, and wondering what I would say if I was. Not for the first time I recognized what a complex figure Westlake was; what I saw as his bravery and tenacity, he would see as a simple dedication to his role as a historian. He had a very basic self confidence that made him comfortable to be around, but though he was an academic, I had no doubt that he could handle himself in a scuffle.

"In the article Kincaid gives an approximate location," I said. "Couldn't we do a thorough search in our own time?"

As much as I loved the idea of going back, it made sense that doing it in present time would allow us to significantly upgrade our equipment, and there would be no time restrictions.

"That would be the best way to start our search except for one major problem; that part of the park has been closed to the public for years. I'm told that not even park employees are allowed in that area," he explained.

Upon hearing that, I felt the slightest little tingle on the back of my neck. This was getting interesting. "So what's our plan?"

"Well first of all, your beard is coming in nicely," he said. He'd asked me to stop shaving three weeks earlier. "But those Buddy Holly style horned rimmed glasses are too modern for 1909, so I went to your eye doctor and had him make these for you."

He handed me a pair of wire rimmed glasses...the kind my friends called Granny Glasses.

"You can keep your hair long, but we'll cut it back so that it's not down to your shoulders."

Hannah appeared with some clothing from the period, complete with a wide brimmed frontier hat and boots. The clothes looked beat up and worn, as befitting someone who had been living outdoors for a while. My eyes lit up to see that there was also a pistol in its own holster.

Westlake, seeing my reaction to the weapon, said this: "It's a Colt .45 Peacemaker. It's filled with blanks, but as I removed the firing pin, it couldn't shoot a real bullet if you wanted it to. I'm not expecting us to encounter any trouble, but if you're going to look like someone used to rough country, you'll need to be armed. Now go put that stuff on."

I did as instructed, pausing to check myself out in the bathroom mirror. I looked pretty good. Minus the thick glasses, I might have been able to pass for a young gun in one of the many outlaw gangs that still roamed much of the West in the 1890's. I sneered at my reflection, trying to affect a tougher look. I tried drawing the gun and found it to be a little heavier than I thought, making a quick, smooth draw difficult. After a few attempts though, I felt as if I didn't look totally ridiculous. Don't mess with the skinny kid wearing glasses, he's a stone cold killer. Feeling like I fit the part a little better, I swaggered back out to the picnic table. Hannah looked a little surprised but said simply, "yes."

Westlake looked me up and down for a moment and said, "It's good, but a couple of suggestions come to mind. First, tone back the hard ass attitude by twenty percent. Your instincts are spot on, you never want to look like an easy target, but you also don't want to encourage a challenge from anyone. I want you to look more like the drug dealer in Seattle, cool headed and competent. And secondly, the way you're wearing the Colt, down at your side...that's mostly a concoction of Hollywood. Most men of the period wore their handgun in front at their waist. It really allows for a much quicker draw. Not that you'll be doing any of that."

I adjusted the gun belt as per his instructions, and found it a more comfortable arrangement. I turned away from them and practiced a draw. The gun came out quickly and smoothly on the first pull; *Mikey the Kid.*

"Alright, let's get something to eat, and then try to get a good night's sleep. We leave in the morning," Westlake announced.

"You still haven't told me yet where we're going," I said. I doubted I would sleep much, but knowing our destination might help me.

"We're going to a small mining town called Williams. It's about sixty miles from the south rim of the Canyon. During my last trip, I learned that it was here, not in Phoenix, that Kincaid told his story to the writer of the article, who then sold it to the Gazette. I will pose as a prospector and you will be my hired hand. We have fallen on hard times, so we are up for any kind of news about the gold finds in the area, or employment of any kind. I will portray you as a very quiet man. You will do nothing to contradict that. If you are asked a direct question, give the shortest possible answer. If you'd like to affect a stutter, I'm fine with that. It's been my experience that people are uncomfortable having lengthy conversations with people they see as diminished."

Somehow I'd just gone from hardened gun hand to stuttering gimp, but I had absolute trust in his attention to detail, so I was completely on board. That attention to detail had him handing me a small purse.

"In there you'll find a ten dollar gold piece, and some smaller currency. You probably won't need it, but you're covered if you do. Just so you know, you're carrying about three hundred dollars in today's currency, so use it carefully if you need to use it at all."

I looked at the coins and cash, and wondered what he had paid to buy coinage of that time...but then he was Westlake, and I didn't ask those questions.

The last thing we did before sleeping was this; Westlake and I posed for a picture, taken by Hannah in our frontier garb, him looking totally at ease, also bearded, and looking like a movie star, but in the same beat up clothes I was wearing.

I wish I still had the shot now, but when I finally saw it, I thought this: Butch Cassidy and the Dumbass Kid.

12

Play It Again Sam

*"I ain't gonna take none of your foolin' around, I
ain't gonna take none of your putting' me down"*
Screamin' Jay Hawkins

*"You mess with me, we have a problem, you mess
with my family, I cut out your heart and feed it to my
dogs."*
Unnamed crime boss (and apparent owner of dogs)

We were up early, Hannah shepherding us through
breakfast and into the backyard, towards the fountain.
Unlike the night before, the big chair was once again in
place. It had been years since I'd last seen it, and I was
instantly stressed. Westlake, as always, was relaxed and
matter of fact and that put me almost at ease, but it
took some talking by him to get me leveled out.

"This should be an easy one," he said. "It's not like
we're going to a place where you can't speak the
language. Just remember that when we get there, you'll
be disoriented and trying to catch your breath. Just take
a deep breath and you'll be fine."

And so with that I sat in the chair, he stood behind
me, and we were gone. It was black and then white and
I was bent over and trying to catch my breath.

The first thing I noticed was the sound of birds and the bright sunshine. We were in a small clearing in the midst of a tall pine forest. The air was crisp and clean and the temperature on this March morning in the year 1909, felt about fifty degrees. Though I was not here to see the Beatles, I felt a similar excitement and energy. I was apparently bug eyed and walking in circles, because Westlake put a hand on my shoulder and said quietly, "breathe and relax".

During the last month, it was a technique he used to get me to focus on slowing my breathing down to begin meditation. It worked and I could feel my shoulders drop down into a more relaxed position.

"That's better. Now this is what I want you to believe: we've camped about a mile outside of town. We've come up on horseback from Phoenix. It's about a hundred and seventy miles and it took us about a week. We're giving, not only ourselves, but the horses, a break by walking into town."

Through the trees, I spied a well-worn dirt road. The idea of us having a 'back story' made perfect sense, and it allowed me to feel more a part of this time frame. Westlake was, as always, meticulous.

"We're about a ten minute walk from town, and when we get there, we will rent a room at the Harvey House hotel. We will then eat a leisurely lunch in the hotel lobby. At some point, we will head across to The Cabinet Saloon. Much of what happens after that we will play by ear. Our time limit in this place is no more than seventy-two hours. Are you ready?"

I nodded and we began the short walk to town. I could smell it well before we got there; as a mixture of burning coal, livestock, and cooking food smells hung in the air. We rounded a corner and made our way up a small rise, and the town appeared in the distance. Westlake said that, as it was the closest town to the Canyon, it had recently started touting itself as The Gateway to the Grand Canyon. It looked like that promo was working; the town was humming with activity. As we walked the last few hundred yards to the town, Westlake told me that the railroad from Williams to the Canyon had started eight years earlier, and that the town was in the midst of a tourist boom the likes of which it had never seen.

"It's been great for business, but it brought all the problems that come with being a booming frontier town; prostitution, crime, and even an opium den. You also have wealthy tourists rubbing elbows with miners, prospectors, and ranch hands. It's not always a happy mix but it won't last long, the automobile will, in time, send this place back to obscurity. By the time the town gets to our era, there will be talk about restarting the railroad, but more for nostalgic reasons."

When he said that, I felt the same sadness that I felt when I'd met the Beatles in a time jump years before; none of these people knew their future, but I did, and it made them somehow precious to me.

The town itself looked more modern than I thought it would, but our clothes were quite right. We fit in perfectly, not the poorest guys in town, but certainly not amongst the wealthy. Much of the town was made up of buildings made of brick, and the signage was reasonably modern in some cases. There were horses tied to rails, but surprisingly to me, there was also an automobile parked near a rail that would normally have been used for horses. There were a couple people checking out the car, but it didn't seem like a big surprise in the town.

"They're coming," Westlake said, as we walked past the brand new example of an ancient (to us) artifact.

We walked, through a crowded street, to the Harvey House hotel. Westlake booked the room. After putting our few things in it, we headed down to eat some food. Westlake ordered for us and this is how it happened:

Big guy waiter, "What do you want?"

Westlake, "We'll both have the steak and potatoes."

Big guy waiter, looking at me: "You don't talk?"

Westlake," He doesn't talk much."

Big guy waiter, grinning at me, "Is he dumb? Sometimes quiet equals dumb."

Westlake, "Quiet no more equals dumb, than talkative equals smart."

The last was delivered with an arched eyebrow that made the big man smirk, bow elaborately, and walk away. "What an asshole," Westlake said under his breath.

Before long, the big man brought our food, placed it on the table, and after scowling at Westlake, departed. We ate and watched the town go by. It was, to me, like watching an excellent period piece movie, but Westlake was into the moment, and he noticed me picking at my food.

"My experience in travel is this: gorge yourself with food and water, and then do more of the same. This is your chance to eat lots of everything. It will allow us to be strong while we're here, and we won't show up back at home so burnt out. That would piss off Hannah...we can't do that."

So we ate, traded stories, (his were better than mine), and at some point we walked down 'Saloon Row' as it was called, to a joint called the Cabinet Saloon. We walked in and saw a mid-afternoon activity already in place. It was an odd combination of what appeared to

3 OF A KIND!

be hard core gamblers, ranch hands, and well to do folks in there for a drink, killing time before the train came in.

Westlake walked us straight to the poker table. "You're up," he said.

"Huh," I said, way too loudly.

"I know you can play," he said quietly to me. "I want you in this game. I think that's Kincaid to your left." With that he announced my entrance to the game by saying, "my buddy will take that seat."

Two things about this: first, Westlake 'knowing I could play' came from me bragging to him about winning a drunken poker night with some equally drunken friends.

Second, the fact that he named and identified the man we were looking for as being to my left, made it almost impossible for me to look away from him. He was an imposing figure; middle aged, well over six feet, cleared eyed, and with every bit the look of 'the adventurer' the article claimed him to be. I heard a man on his other side call him George. So he was George Kincaid, otherwise known as G.E. Kincaid.

The game started, and to my surprise, of my five cards, I was dealt a pair of jacks. I watched as everyone but Kincaid checked. He raised it a dollar (a large amount by my reckoning of that time period) and the other three players dropped out.

Figuring that he too has a pair, I matched his dollar, getting a nod from Westlake. We both discarded three cards and were both dealt three more cards. I became lost in the poker moment when, of my three new cards,

I was dealt another jack. I remembered what Westlake had told me about the relative value of the money I was carrying, and raised Kincaid another dollar.

By now there was, by that time's present buying value, about sixty dollars' worth up for grabs, so it was not a small pot. I figured George had at least a high pair of something, but then I saw him blink, and I knew that my three of anything was going to beat his pair of whatever. I made a loud noise at winning the big pot when Kincaid folded, which immediately had Westlake at my shoulder. While smiling and appearing to congratulate me, he whispered, "start losing. " This confused me no end, but I did my best, over the next few hours, to lose without being too obvious.

I remained quiet, giving grunts or non-committal shrugs when asked a question, an approach that some, even today, consider a good strategy in poker. Kincaid, however, was a talker. I didn't sense that he was a bragger, it was more that he was gregarious, friendly, and he knew he'd been to many places us greenhorns would never see. Westlake had bought the table a round of drinks after my initial victory, and continued to periodically keep them coming. George at one point said with a smile to Westlake, "you're gonna have to get me a lot drunker if you want your boy to win."

The afternoon turned into evening, and playing carefully, I managed to slowly lose most of the large pot I'd won hours earlier. Throughout the game, Kincaid kept up a running commentary on a number of different subjects; from poker, to hunting and trapping, to prospecting. Since we were supposedly prospectors, Westlake took the opportunity to say this to Kincaid:

"So Mike and I came up here from Phoenix hoping to get into the Canyon and do a little prospecting, only to find out, that a few months ago, it became illegal to gold pan. Is that right George? Did they close the whole Canyon off to mining?"

Kincaid gave Westlake an amused look and said, "Yes, they did. So it looks like you boys came a long way for nothing. But if I were you two, I might stick around for a bit. There's some big news about to break that may change everything. Two fit men, such as yourselves, might be able to find some extended work hauling some things out of the Canyon."

"What kind of big news?" Westlake asked.

Just then, an anxious looking, well-dressed man walked up behind Kincaid, put his hand on his shoulder, and said, "George, could I speak to you for a moment in private?"

Kincaid gave the man an irritated look and said, "Not now Sam, can't you see I'm playing poker?"

Sam? Could this be the S.A. Jordan mentioned in the article?

Sam persisted, "It's important, George." He then looked at the rest of us around the table with some suspicion.

"Alright boys," George said, slapping his cards on the table. "Deal me out. We don't want Sam here to piss himself."

With that the two men walked out the back door.

"Let's go Mikey," Westlake said. "I guess you've lost enough of our grub stake for one night."

We walked out the front door. When we got outside, Westlake said in a hushed voice, "I'm going to head around back. You head around the other side. If you get questioned, you're looking for the outhouse. But keep your ears open...something's not right."

Westlake moved down the left hand side of the building, and I moved carefully, in the dark, down the right hand side. When I got to the back, I heard some muffled but angry sounding voices a little further on. I hunched down and followed a chest high fence that led in the direction of the voices. They were right on the other side of the fence when I stopped to listen.

"Jesus, George, tell me you didn't just do that? I thought we were going to keep this quiet until the right time," the man called Sam said, his voice starting to rise.

"I'm not responsible for how or what you think," George replied with an even voice. "I never agreed to that. And it's my discovery, I only brought you in because you claim to be a scientist!"

"I am a scientist damn it! But there are ways to release this information, when and if it becomes necessary!" Sam was almost yelling now.

"If it becomes necessary? What the hell is that supposed to mean?" George was now also getting angry.

"Well no matter that, I didn't know you were going to talk to a reporter! How the hell am I going to quiet this thing down?"

Sam and George were obviously not on the same page.

"Now listen to me you dolt," George said carefully through gritted teeth, "if I want to stand on top of this building and shout it to the world, I will do exactly that, and neither you nor the fucking Bureau will stop me! "

Then things started happening in rapid succession. I heard the unmistakable sound of a gun clearing its holster, as Sam said, "I'm sorry George. " He then yelled out, "Tiny, come here!"

I looked around the fence and saw Sam pointing his gun at a dumbfounded George, just as the big waiter came out of the darkness holding a knife at Westlake's throat.

"I found him spying on you," Tiny said. (Is there ever a guy named Tiny who's actually little?)

"God damn it!" Sam barked. "Well there's nothing to be done about it. We'll have to bring him along too. Now where's that kid who was with him? "

I stepped from behind the fence, pushed my gun against the back of his head, and said, "He's right behind you. Now drop the gun and tell the ape to put the knife away."

Tiny sneered and said, "I think that kid would shit hisself afore he'd pull the trigger."

Thinking that Tiny was probably right, I started hyperventilating, and I think Sam was about to call my bluff, when Westlake, still with a knife at his throat said, "Mikey, don't do it, don't kill him! You've already got one hanging over your head. We don't want to be running from another one! "

The fact that Westlake was painting me as a sociopathic killer, oddly enough, made me relax. With the gun still pointed at the back of Sam's head, I pulled the hammer back. In the silence, it made a loud click. Then in my best Clint Eastwood voice, I said, "how about it, asshole, should I spread your brains all over the back yard?"

Sam sighed deeply, dropped the gun, and said, "Put the knife down Tiny."

Tiny released Westlake, and sheathed the knife. I stepped back and with hands shaking almost uncontrollably, had difficulty putting my gun back in its holster.

George, who'd been quiet as this last bit of drama had played out, picked up Sam's gun, and said "you and I are obviously done, but I'm going to give you some free advice: the next time you pull a gun on me, it will be the last thing you do, for I will surely kill you."

With that he whipped the butt of the pistol across Sam's jaw, and as Sam fell unconscious, he turned and threw the gun into the woods.

Tiny, seeing that, started to move towards George, but Westlake jumped between them with raised his fists, saying to Tiny, "Put 'em up."

Tiny almost laughed out loud and took a big roundhouse swing which Westlake ducked under, while punching his right fist deep into Tiny's belly. As Tiny bent over with a gasp, Westlake brought his left fist around to clip Tiny behind his right ear. Tiny went down and out, leaving Westlake standing there, relaxed as if he had just bent down to tie his shoe.

I was leaning against the fence, trying not to throw up, when George stepped up to shake my hand. "I think I was about done for if you hadn't come along. Sam wouldn't have had the sack to do it, but the ape would've. I can't say as I've ever had anyone let me win at poker, and save my life in the same night. I don't know about you, but I need a drink. This time I'm buying. Now who did you say you two are again?"

A short time later, the three of us sat with a bottle of whiskey at a table. George told us about his discovery in the Canyon, and about how he'd told a reporter the whole tale, and that it was soon going to be in the Gazette. Though we knew the printed details well, hearing about it first hand was jaw dropping.

He told us of the countless rooms cut into the caves and all the amazing things they contained, including tombs, golden images, and hieroglyphs. One thing George added that was new to us was that he took numerous photographs, some by flashlight, of the items in the cave. "I gave them to that snake Sam Jordan, so who knows what became of them. He was supposed to send them to the Smithsonian, but I'm guessing that never happened. It just occurred to me that Sam was very interested in the statues, especially the ones made of gold. I know that he's a professor, but maybe he's also just a common god damn thief."

It was easy to like George, and as I sat there and listened to his description of all he had discovered, it occurred to me that I was getting drunk. I also realized with a sudden shock that what obviously really happened that night, without Westlake and I there to interfere, was that Sam and Tiny must have waylaid George and then done God knows what to him.

As I looked across at George, him sitting there, large as life, I remembered Westlake telling me years before that we couldn't change anything in a time line. When we interfere, we think we are changing things, only to find, upon our return, that history hadn't changed. Westlake's theory was that perhaps our involvement bumped that narrative into another time line. So as I looked across at George, I tried not to see him as a dead man; I tried to see him as a man living on in another time line; the one we'd just created. In spite of that I grabbed his hand, another sacred soul, and said, "You're a good man George Kincaid."

Westlake looked at George and said simply, "I agree." He then stood up and said, "It's been a long, crazy day, and we have plans for the morning, so Mike and I have to say goodnight."

We'd learned what we came to find out; the story was true, though who knew why it never officially came to light. As Cyndi Lauper once said, 'money changes everything.' We stood up, shook hands, and left our somewhat puzzled new friend and headed back to our hotel room.

We got there and gathered our few things. Westlake was getting ready to blink us out of there, but I couldn't get over the story being true. "We could have George tell us where the place is, or maybe even take us there. Wouldn't it be incredible to see all that stuff?!"

Westlake turned and looked at me and said this:

"First of all, Mike, that was a brave thing you did back there. I don't know how many people could've stepped into that situation knowing they had a gun that wouldn't shoot and do what you did. You played it perfectly. That was an all of nothing bluff. I know now that I should have trusted you with a real gun...maybe if there is a next time. Second of all, we don't know why a follow-up on that story never happened. There could be a number of reasons, and none of them are good. What we do know is that men were willing to kill other men to cover it up. Now that we know it's true, maybe there's another way to approach the story, but as for now, I'm not willing to put my life at risk, and certainly not yours, to investigate the story any further. We've been here long enough."

With that he said, almost to himself, "goodbye Williams, Arizona." And we were gone.

Black...loud humming noise...white...trying to catch my breath...home.

13

Far Flung Travels

"People who see nobility in rooting for The Team That Never Wins have never understood that most of us have no choice; we were just born under a bad sign and got what we got."
Steven King on being a Red Sox fan prior to 2004

"You hit one of my guys, I'm taking down two of yours----you tell Clemens that!"
Pedro Martinez yelling to the Yankees dugout during the '03 American League Championship Series

"I am the player to be named later."
Crash Davis from *Bull Durham*

"The Red Sox Are World Champions!" screamed the drunken fellow to my left, before blowing into a red plastic horn until his eyes bulged. It was ten o'clock on the morning of October 30, 2004, the day of <u>the</u> Victory Parade. I capitalized that because while there had already been a couple of parades in recent years for the New England Patriots, this was the one New Englanders had been anticipating for eighty-six frigging years. At that point, I'd already had a couple drinks, and it was about the happiest few days of my life.

My own personal hit parade of happy days goes like this:

No.1. My daughter Sara was born.

No.2. The Red Sox win their first championship in 86 years.

No.3. Everything else.

And here I was standing along the Victory Parade route with an estimated three million(!) people, some standing twenty deep, watching the first of the duck boats carrying the players go by. This was uncharted territory in these parts, grown men and women were weeping, some holding up pictures of dead relatives so that they too could see the players go by. The joke for years had been that a Red Sox World Championship would signal the final days of humanity.

In the crowd, I saw a man who I thought was Steven King. Like many of the people there, he was glassy eyed and disheveled, as if he hadn't slept since the series ended three days earlier. As the first duck boat went by carrying Manny Ramirez, Curt Schilling, and a wildly grinning Pedro Martinez, the Steven King guy said loudly to no one in particular, "make peace with whatever God you truck with, be he goat headed thunderclap or naked wanderer, for the end of all things is near."

It was that kind of day; when all past Red Sox crimes and debts were marked paid and forgiven. A stake was finally driven in the dark heart of the memories that had tortured the fan base for years. Gone was the pain of the '48 loss to the Indians which had maimed my Dad. Gone was the misery of the '78 one game playoff loss to the hated Yankees and with it Bucky fucking

Dent. And finally gone was the abject despair that followed the ball going through poor cursed Bill Buckner's legs in '86. They were replaced with a boundless jubilation that bordered on nirvana. If you've never hung out in a love fest with three million people, I must tell you, it's unforgettable, and don't take my word for it...ask any Chicago Cubs fan. They recently ended a one hundred and eight year draught.

As I stumbled around Boston, lost in a reverie of sports bliss, I remembered that I had a day or so to recover, and then it was off to Mongolia...seriously, Mongolia.

Maybe it was fitting that my love of music, and travel, were both fueled by my (mostly) life long journey with The Fools. And a word about those Fools now if you don't mind...but you've come this far, so here goes. Do you hang out with friends who support you no matter what? I do. Do you have friends who watch you climb out on a questionable limb and follow you out? I do. Do you have friends who at some point realize that the limb is untenable and then cut it off, with you still on it? I do, and as I've said before, if we weren't in a band, we'd find another reason to hang out.

But all that aside, over the years my life as a fool had allowed me to travel a good part of the world, through the US, Canada, Europe, and Japan, a continuing journey that even Mr. Westlake might have cheered.

Anyhow, a friend had hipped me to a company out of Boston called Far Flung Tours. They needed someone who had traveled a lot and would be willing to talk endlessly about things he knew nearly nothing about. The band was on a break so I was their man.

So it was that as I was about to head towards Mongolia, on a trip that would supposedly spur Boston folks to travel to that unusual destination. I was told by someone who'd done it that, in order to be taken seriously, I would need to be accompanied by someone the locals would see as a servant. "Huh," I thought. And then it occurred to me, me who'd always had a protective barrier throughout my performing life, me who had, at times, put other people in harm's way in order that I got to do what I wanted to do on stage. I knew what I needed; I needed a roadie.

There was only one choice. First however let me say that there should be a special place, an Arlington Cemetery type place, adjacent to the Rock and Roll Hall of Fame that honors roadies. These are people who, for reasons even us band members can't quite figure out, give up real jobs to travel the world like gypsies, in support of exciting, but essentially unstable personalities who at times put those roadie's wellbeing at risk.

My immediate choice for this well paid job, for both of us, was Fred Mozdziez. We called Fred 'number 7' and the joke was that he was the seventh best roadie we'd ever had. Fred, younger than us Fools, grew up in Ipswich at a time when the band was getting nonstop radio play in all the regional markets, and for better or not, Fred thought we were the friggin nuts.

Though he would become an electrician, and later a union head in Boston, he spent nearly every available moment working for the band. I say 'working' but he never took a penny from us. We tried many times to pay him, even to sticking money in his pockets, only to find that he'd spend the money buying us gift certificates to a restaurant. Though we called him number 7, Fred was the best roadie we ever had.

And fine you say, but Jesus, Mike what about the Mongolian thing that you mentioned a few hundred friggin' words ago!? Okay, let's get to that!

The deal was this; Fred and I were to fly to Paris, and then take a connecting flight to Ulan Bator, the capital of Mongolia. There we would meet our interpreter, rest for a day, and fly the last leg of our journey about five hundred miles south to the small town of Dolanzadgad. So over the course of almost three days, we would be spending about twenty-five hours in the air. Even for someone accustomed to travel, this was no small feat, but for Fred it was an ordeal. While I'd have a drink, put the ear buds in and fall asleep, Fred, who wasn't a drinker, would fidget. When not fidgeting, he was practicing phrases in his newly acquired Mongolian to English phrase book.

"Baktai noolay onchu dabuzaydak," he would say to me triumphantly, and then pause with an eyebrow raised, as if I might understand.

"And...," I would say, "...what does that mean?"

"It means, my hovercraft is filled with eels," Fred replied with a laugh. Number 7 was a big Monty Python fan.

"Well that's a phrase that should come in handy," I said. When not fidgeting or reading from his phrase book, he would ask me questions.

"Number 1, how much more time do you think it'll be?" Fred called me Number 1; his response to being called Number 7. Like a preschooler, Fred was asking me this about once an hour.

"I don't know, Fred, probably a few more hours til Paris. Why don't you try and get some sleep."

The tour company, wanting to put us in the least possible discomfort, had placed us in first class. We had room to stretch out and the food was pretty good, but Fred was antsy.

"I'm gonna take a little walk," he said, as if he were going to walk a mile on a beach, instead of the length of the plane and back. This was Fred's third 'little walk.'

I awoke after a bit to find the seat next to mine empty, so I got up, stretched, and took my own little walk. I didn't see him until I got towards the end of the plane. He was sitting next to an older woman and had a small child jumping up and down in his lap. Older women always tended to like Fred, he was the handsome, polite kind of guy you hoped your daughter would marry, as opposed to me...the one you hoped she avoided.

"Number 1, this is Sheila," he said, nodding at the woman, "and this is her granddaughter Shelley." Sheila smiled politely but Shelley was not impressed and went back to jumping up and down on Fred.

"And guess where they're going?" Fred asked.

"I don't know," I replied, "...um....Paris?"

"Yup," Fred said, as if there could be another answer.

"I've been talking his ear off, and he's such a dear with his advice and concern," Sheila said, beaming at Fred.

Fred's own relationships with women were often complicated. He tended to fall in love with the broken types, and then spend all of his time trying to fix them, until they would eventually get bored and break his heart. Despite that, he never lost his faith in people. Fred was a good human.

"So Fred tells me you're a rock star?" The fact that she said it in the form of a question spoke volumes. I'd often gotten this reaction from first meetings with club owners, who were convinced I was a roadie, not the lead singer of the band they'd hired.

"Fred exaggerates," I replied.

Sheila seemed ok with that answer and then resumed her conversation with Fred. There was some talk about her troubled son in law, and how her daughter was under appreciated by him. Fred spent the rest of the flight consoling and advising, totally in his element, and I went back to sleep.

"When do you think he'll come?" Fred asked.

We'd been waiting at the Ulan Bator airport for almost two hours, and there was still no sign of our guide/interpreter. Fred was holding up a sign that said **Girard** and waving it hopefully at anyone who walked by.

"How would I know that, Fred?" I said a bit testily.

We had no number to call, so all we could do was wait. Finally, a young man came in, saw us and the sign, and walked quickly over to us. He was wearing a Boston t-shirt (the band not the town) under a jean jacket and seemed delighted to see us. He quickly took the sign from Fred, handed it to me, and shook Fred's hand up and down.

"Mr. Girard," he said in pretty good English, "it's a pleasure to meet you! My name is Batu Khan. I'm told you're a rock star from Boston. I'm so sorry to be late, but as we say in Mongolia, my horse had different plans."

Fred gave a slightly embarrassed bow, dislodged his hand, and said, "No, mini daygla bowneese dap number 7," he replied to Batu. "This is Mr. Girard," he said, turning to me.

Batu frowned a bit. "Why does your red dog have a number seven on it?"

Fred looked puzzled, unclear that his Mongolian was a tad flawed.

Batu recovered and shook my hand with a warm smile.

"We are going to have the best time," he said while waving to a porter to take our bags.

As we walked out of the airport to the adjacent parking lot, Batu kept up a steady, but wandering dialogue. "It's good that you came at this season. It's not cold like winter. The hotel tonight is good but tomorrow in Dolanzadgad is not so good. The festival however we go to is fucking fantastic."

He turned to see if we noted his appropriate use of an American curse word. We got to his 'horse' which was an older jeep, filled it with our bags and climbed in. As my servant, Fred handled the tipping and sat in front with Batu, while I sat in back. It took some groaning from the car and some cursing in his native tongue from Batu, but it finally started. While we drove, Batu corrected Fred's earlier slaughter of his language, but commended his attempt.

"No visitor ever tries to speak our language. Keep trying, my people will love you for it."

The hotel wasn't far away, and soon we were in the lobby making plans to meet in the morning. Before we parted, Fred looked at Batu's shirt and asked, "Are you a Boston fan?"

"Best band in the world," Batu replied with some reverence. He then sang a bit of *'More than a Feeling'* in a high quavering voice. It was like hearing the song sung by a temple singer in a mosque.

"Mike knows Brad Delp," Fred blurted out.

"Mr. Brad Delp?" Batu gasped as he put both palms together and bowed with a slight nod of wonder. Ah, the power of rock n roll. "He is truly a rock god," Batu said reverently.

Our flight to Dolanzadgad was uneventful. It's a small city, even by Mongolian standards, with a population of about fifteen thousand. It was the first time I'd ever traveled in an aircraft with goats and chickens wandering the aisles. Fred tried again to use his limited knowledge of Mongolian to Batu's amusement.

"He just told that older gentleman with the goat that we were traveling to Dolanzadgad to skip rope. He then tried to tell the man that he liked his goat, but he used a verb that was too strong. It suggested something inappropriate with the goat." That explained what I saw, the man moving his goat to the inside seat, away from the smiling but obviously insane American.

We were flying to the far flung city because of the annual hot pepper festival, a three day event that brought in people from all over the region, many by horse. The horse culture is still prevalent and on our first day we were treated to some amazing riders performing acrobatic tricks with uncanny accuracy using bow and arrow from atop a speeding horse. Let's not forget that it was this tribe of horseman and yak herders, that in the thirteenth century under the leadership of Genghis Khan, conquered most of the land from China to Hungary! That is still a standing square mile record in the Planet Domination Game...take that Adolf!

I found the Mongolian people to be warm and friendly, and with a fondness for very spicy food. I have friends who keep outrageously hot peppers in the house, just in case they wanted to challenge someone's love of hot stuff. The Mongolians would laugh at them. They eat peppers daily that would fry the nuts off of most of us casual hot pepper lovers. Insane

Why the name of the town itself roughly translates to 'eat fire--pee blood.' While I was there I met people who had eaten so many hot peppers that their scorched vocal chords would barely allow them to talk above a whisper. I even met a man whose love of the molten veggie had burned a hole in the roof of his mouth, and because of this he was able to stick his tongue out through his nose! Take that you '80's coke freaks!

In my short stay, mostly helped by Batu, I made friends and learned about the potency of the local beverage--fermented yak's milk. This is an ass kicking beverage that seems to combine the properties of good scotch and psychedelic mushrooms. Perhaps it has to do with what the wandering beasts eat, but I soon felt the effects and I was glad to have Number 7 along, if only to help keep me focused and upright.

Fred was his charming smiling self throughout, completely sober in that drunken stoned mass of people, and totally inflating my, and The Fools place, in rock history.

Yes, we were popular on the east coast, and we'd toured North America for years backing up some of the biggest bands in the world. We'd also had success in Germany and France, and inexplicably, Japan. Yes we'd had songs that charted nationally, but we are to rock what Crash Davis was to baseball in Bull Durham (Google it). He was the all-time leader in minor league home runs, but only spent twenty-one days in the major leagues.   Fred however made us sound like the American Beatles.

I noticed that despite his foreign mannerisms, the locals really took a liking to Fred, especially the women. He tried out his phrases on them, leading to much laughter, and some obvious confusion.

It was on our third day there that the culmination of the festival happened. It was a well-attended event and it went like this:

All the tribal leaders were expected to take a mouth full of the local savagely hot peppers, and then, one at a time, they are expected to recount some heroic tale of

Mongolia's past. Apparently, the only way these poor men can get through this is to get whacked out on the local beverage prior to eating the peppers. What follows during the story telling is an amazing array of crying, hand waving and gasping, much to the applause and delight of all in attendance. It's all done in a good natured way, the audience gets to see their chiefs in some distress and yet, they are still expected to deliver a story.

Imagine my surprise, when I was fully into my third glass of the potent yak concoction, that Batu stood on the small stage and said some words I didn't understand, except for the words Brad Delp, and then Mike Girard. And then to loud applause, he motioned for me to come on stage. Given the situation, I had no choice. Fred was smiling and clapping.

"Fred, you fuck," I yelled at him as I stumbled drunkenly onto the stage. I was handed some peppers, which I only chewed and swallowed because of the frat party type cheering from the few thousand people out there. In my mind, I saw my vocal chords burning and my singing days being over, but I somehow managed to choke them down.

Then, while gasping, crying, and trying not to tip over, I was handed another glass of the evil yak juice. My first thought was 'What the Fuck Am I Doing up Here!' Then I looked out at the expectant throng. The good news was, my days of stage fright were long over. The bad news was, it didn't matter if I had nothing to tell them. Hey, I was on a stage, there must be something I could do. Singing, at the moment, however, was definitely not one of those things.

Trying to breathe and not either throw up, pass out, or go into cardiac arrest, I looked over at Batu, and realized he was waiting for me. "You say it and I will tell them," he said.

I panicked as I had nothing to tell them. Then suddenly while I was gasping and crying, I realized that I had felt this pain before. I'd felt it in '75 and again in '78, and yes in '86, and maybe most painfully in '03 at Yankee Stadium. I began to spin a tale of a star crossed tribe who had suffered many great and countless defeats at the hands of their bitter enemies, the Yanks. Through all of the humbling lost battles though, the tribe never lost heart. And then among this tribe of loveable losers, and in their darkest hour, a group of warrior chiefs arose from their ranks---idiots they called themselves.

There was Manny, who smiled but carried a great and powerful club, and Big Papi, who was fearless and never gave up, and seemed able to do magical things with his war club that terrified the enemy. (I could tell that Papi's description struck a nerve) There was Pedro, who was not large of stature, but very large of heart and able to conjure fireballs from his very fingers, and Tek, a chief who put his fist in the face of even the fiercest enemies, and finally, there was the mighty Schilling (some even said he was related to the great Khan).

It was he that stood tallest when all seemed lost. It was he that, though seriously wounded and bleeding, led the other warriors to a great and final victory over the hated Yanks. By now the crowd was standing and cheering. I named the five great warriors one more time and pumped my fist after each one;

Manny!...Pedro!...Tek!... Schilling!...Every fist in the audience was now raising with mine after every name. Finally I yelled Biggg Papiii!!

The place went nuts and I smiled, wondering if my gums were bleeding. I knew my story was over, and so did Batu, who did a great arm flourish and turned his hand towards me. I attempted the same flourish and felt the stage rushing up to meet my face...and that's the last thing I remember. I hit the deck at the end of my story, apparently not an unusual occurrence at the festival, and was carried off by Fred and Batu to the cheering of the crowd.

Batu said this the next day, "Your speech was very good. The chiefs were inspired. Had we all horses we might have retaken the empire."

My head was throbbing, my throat was raw, and I could painfully feel the entire length of my intestinal track, but I had a sense of relief, as if I'd made it through a hazing, and been asked to join the fraternity. Then I saw Fred's face and knew something was not right.

"What's up?" I asked them both. Batu had an almost philosophical look about him, but Fred looked spooked.

"It was a misunderstanding, Number One," Fred cried out, with some arm waving. He was having a hard time meeting my eyes.

"What happened, Fred?" I asked with a sense of foreboding.

He looked down with arms outstretched, and then looked helplessly at Batu.

"Your man Fred made a promise, on your behalf. You are to be married to a powerful chief's daughter. To be clear he is powerful, not her, but she will be in time." He said this as if it was an enticement.

Fred's eyes were bulging, and he kept saying "Oh, Mike" over and over, while walking in a circle. Him not calling me 'Number One" meant he was totally stressed.

I was too hungover to take this seriously, but Batu explained what would now happen.

"The ceremony will happen this afternoon. While you are an older man, and she is quite young, she is happy to be joined to an American rock star. Fred told her good things about you. She will happily live in the Fools Mansion and bear you many children."

"For Christ fucking sake, Fred! What did you do?" I yelled.

Fred looked lost.

"And Batu," I was still yelling, "how could you let this happen?"

Batu looked at me sheepishly and said, "I may have neglected my duties, but in my defense, he seemed to be getting on well."

Fred took a deep breath and said quietly, "I was telling her about the meeting of two great tribes...I thought she understood."

"He used the word 'debala' which means families, not tribes," Batu said, as if that explained everything. "It seemed that, on your behalf, he was proposing."

"Fred," I said, keeping my voice even, "did you not tell them I was married? And are you going to explain this to Ginny?"

Fred was gasping, like he'd had hot peppers, but Batu said "I do not think he has the skills to speak that."

Batu didn't know my wife Ginny, but he was right on both counts.

"How can I get the hell out of here without insulting the whole country?" I asked.

Batu thought a bit. "I have an idea."

That afternoon we made our way to a large round tent covered with animal skins called a yurt. It's still the traditional dwelling of the nomads in the steppes of Central Asia. Batu told us his plan on the way over.

"This will be delicate. Mike, while I speak, you will look sad, and nod once to the young woman, then you will look at her father and slowly shake your head. Fred, you will look at the floor and say nothing. Are we ready?"

We said we were, paused outside the yurt, and Batu yelled some form of greeting into the tent. A flap was pulled aside, and we entered. It was very cozy; there was a small cooking fire in the center, and quite a lot of living space. There were five people in the room; three older men, a stern looking middle aged woman, and a pretty young woman who might still be a teenager....apparently, my betrothed.

"Jesus, Fred," I said under my breath.

Batu introduced everyone. Her father and two uncles eyed me carefully, probably doubting my ability to ride a horse. Nor was the mother impressed, probably doubting my ability to give her a grandchild. These were both quite reasonable guesses on their part. The young woman, whose name was Khulan, seemed to be trying to put a good face on it, after all, who knew what Fred had told her about the supposedly rich American rocker.

We all sat on piled hides in a circle, and then the yak milk poison was passed around. I declined, to the obvious surprise of the uncles, whose last vision of the American boozer was him drunkenly yelling, while staggering around, and then passing out on a stage. When the small talk ended, Batu stood up, bowed solemnly to our host and began to talk. He spoke first to the young woman. I looked sadly at her and nodded. She looked at Fred, whose gaze had not left the floor since our arrival, and then at me. Then she slowly nodded her head. Next he spoke to the father, who was frowning as if something wasn't quite right. The uncles also were looking at Batu suspiciously, and then back at me. I began to get nervous; who knew what a broken promise meant to these people? Would I be target practice at the next festival?

"They say that in your place, your man must marry the girl," Batu said.

"Wheeeew," Fred exclaimed, wiping the sweat off his brow.

"That means you, Fred," I explained.

"Whaaaat?" Fred asked. "I...I...I..."

"This is a negotiation, so I will try again," Batu said.

I looked at Fred and shrugged. At least he wasn't already married. I always hoped Fred would meet a nice girl, but this wasn't exactly the scenario I had envisioned.

Batu again began to speak and it was at that point, when the tension was building, that Batu after a pause, said something barely above a whisper. Our five hosts looked at me and then each other in momentary shock...and then began to laugh. It was a giggle at first, but soon they were laughing really hard, one of the uncles until tears came down his face. I couldn't help but laugh too and that's how the next few minutes went. Fred was the only one not laughing. He was just staring at the floor, and probably praying that the laughter was good news.   After we calmed back down, Batu apparently said our goodbyes for us and we turned to leave, but not without one last outburst of giggling.

In the car on the way back to our hotel, I thanked Batu for his handling of the delicate matter. Even Fred was smiling again.

After a moment I said, "So what did you tell them?"

"I told them a long story. I said that you were a very kind man. A man who had traveled the world and seen many things. An example of your kindness and worldliness was your hiring of the gantaloo, Fred," he explained.

"What does gantaloo mean?" I asked.

"It means small brain...um...what you call simpleton. They had sympathy for Fred to make that mistake."

"Ha!" I said, "Fred, my gantaloo!"

Fred was smirking but I knew he was relieved.

"So why were we all laughing?" I asked. I started chuckling again just thinking about it.

"Well, when they heard that Fred was simple, they were understanding, but they were not entirely over the idea of a rich American rocker marrying their daughter. So I told them that such a marriage for you was impossible."

"Because I'm already married right? They would certainly understand that."

"No," Batu replied. "In this country, it's not unheard of for a powerful man to take a second wife, so I couldn't tell them that."

"Then what did you tell them?" I asked.

"I told them that you liked men...that you were gay."

Fred barked a loud 'HA' and he and Batu giggled, like nitwits most of the way back to the hotel.

It turns out that the Mongolians are a quite tolerant people. They had no issue with me supposedly being gay, but the thought of my servant traveling the world with me and innocently trying set me up with women tickled their funny bones.

The next day Fred and I were on the plane headed home, with promises to each other that certain parts of our story would remain untold...but it was a long time ago...in Mongolia.

14

Returning Japanese

"Travel far enough and you'll meet yourself."
David Mitchell

"The method of learning Japanese, recommended by experts, is to be born as a Japanese baby, raised by a Japanese family, in Japan. And even then it's not easy"
Dave Barry

"How much longer till we get to Tokyo, Number one?" Fred asked as he finished the sandwich he had brought for the flight.

He had planned on eating it about halfway through our fifteen hour trip but in true Fred fashion, he got bored an hour in and ate the entire thing. I was prepared for this, for much like travelling with an amped up four year old, I'd brought a bag full of things that I thought would keep Fred, if not happy, at least occupied. He was now very much involved with an Etch-a-Sketch. Fred was, in his real life, a master electrician, so please don't think I'm painting him as a dummy, he was a smart man. His almost obsessive hobby though was being a Fools roadie and also being my man Friday on trips that I was hired to take. It was a relationship that we both enjoyed, although this trip had a bit of a different vibe, as we were heading there at the request of a Japanese family.

"Well Fred," I said, ever the patient dad, "we've probably got about another fourteen hours left. What are you making?"

Fred had laboriously used the little magnet to make the metal flakes say *The Fools*. Fred carefully handed it over to me, of course keeping it flat. To buy myself another forty minutes of near peace, I took it from him carefully, and as if to get a better look at his creation, I held the thing vertically in front of me. All the metal flakes fell to the bottom. Yes, I admit, I am a dick.

"Ah shit, Fred, I'm sorry. I haven't used one of those in years. What I saw of it looked pretty good, can you make it again?"

Fred, with a big sigh, took it back from me and said, "Of course Number one."

I could do no wrong in Fred's eyes; he would forever be an Ipswich boy, and we would forever be an Ipswich band who almost made it big. In his mind we carried that banner wherever we went. So while he got back to work on his masterpiece, I had a little time to re-think the reason for our trip to Japan.

The year was 2005. It was twenty-five years earlier that we Fools had made a short but eventful trip to Japan in support of our single, *Psycho Chicken*, which had become a minor hit over there. (Once again, to read about this and other early Fools adventures, find 'Psycho Chicken and other Foolish Tales' at Amazon.com)

Over the couple weeks we were there, our guide, and EMI rep, Shigenori (or Shiggy as we called him) had treated us like family, taken the band around the country, and generally bonded with us. While the trip was a blast, it was a little ego deflating for me. At our only press conference back then, the Japanese rock n' roll press seemed to delight in the fact that we Fools, or *Orakamonos* as they called us, had three blond band members. Rich, Stacey, and Chris were soon known as *Sanban kinpatsu no hito*; the blond men. Was I then called *Okashii no hito*, the funny man? No, that's what they called Doug, the bass player. I was called *Mohitori no otoko*...the other guy. Fans and press alike seemed to fall in love with Gino, our large, bald, road manager. *Hageatama* they called him...the bald one...*Hagi* for short.

When our short stay ended, Shiggy brought his pregnant wife, some uncles, some cousins, and some friends to see us off at the airport. Some of them carried homemade signs that said things like *Good bye Fools*, and *Sayonara Golden Ones*. Shiggy seemed to think that our minor impact upon Japan should have resulted in us receiving much more attention. He took it personally and must have decided that we should have a loud send off, even if he had to create one. It was both ridiculous and touching at the same time.

Much like Fred years later, Shiggy thought of our place in rock n roll as being much more elevated than it actually was. But when some people keep telling you how great you are, at some point you stop arguing and go along for the ride.

As we got on the plane to head home back then, I remember thinking "we'll be back soon." But within another year, and after two albums, EMI decided to cut us adrift. As guitar player Rich Bartlett said when asked about the split, "we had a disagreement with EMI, they wanted to get rid of us and we didn't want to go."

Some years passed and we lost touch with our only mainland Japanese friend and supporter.

Sometime in the early two thousands, I googled Shiggy and found that he'd risen through the ranks of record reps and become a big time Japanese showbiz mogul. We Fools, hearing it back then, were happy for him, and tried to think of a way we could finagle our way back there. This was unfortunately well before Facebook, and so even any casual communication was not available at that time. I did learn he'd had a few kids. A few more years passed before we had another Shiggy moment. It was not good and that was what had led to this plane trip. Shiggy's son, Junia, got word to us that Shiggy had passed away.

I was the only one of us Fools able to head back and pay our respects, in large part because I still had contacts with Far Flung Tours so here Fred and I were Japan bound.

When I looked up, Fred was holding a recreation of his Etch-a-Sketch art, and holding it flat in front of me. As I leaned in to see it, he held it up horizontally and again all the metal flakes went to the bottom.

"Ah gee Number one, I'm sorry. I forgot that would happen." Fred was a funny man.

We finally arrived in Tokyo, and as we de-boarded the plane, Fred, who had seemingly talked to half the people on the plane, was saying goodbye to some Italian tourists.

"*CinCin*," Fred said, holding up an imaginary glass to his new friends.

"*CinCin*, Freddy," the tourists said almost in unison, returning the gesture.

"It means ' to your health' in Italian," Fred explained to me. Fred always thought that he had a great talent with foreign tongues, but there was ample evidence to the contrary.

We made our trek through the immense Narita International Airport on our way to collect our baggage. I was pretty much exhausted from the trip, but Fred bounced along, taking in the sights and sounds. Once we'd retrieved our bags, and gone through customs, we headed to a huge 'pick up' area where we were to meet our ride. Like most international airports, there were lots of drivers and limo people holding up signs with the names of the people they were hired to drive.

One sign stood out: it had the word *ORAKAMONOS* written across it in bright colorful letters, and it was held by four young Japanese men. These must be Shiggy's boys, and as we walked towards them, I noticed happily that one of them looked like an exact bespectacled replica of Shiggy twenty-five years later. Two of the other three had hair dyed blond, and the third had shaved his head bald.

We were practically in front of them before Fred's beaming smile must have given us away.

"You must be, Junia," I said to the one with glasses.

His eyes widened and he compared me to a small decades old picture he was holding of The Fools. His face broke into a grin as he said, "Mike!"

Then began the bowings and introductions. All the boys spoke excellent English, and after realizing that Fred was not Rich or Stacey, much to their apparent disappointment, we learned their names. Junia, Juney to his brothers, was obviously the older brother in charge, and he had the same nonstop energy as his dad.

The blond boys were, to my shock, named Richey and Stacey. Richey, upon being introduced, did a short air guitar solo, smiling at Fred and I. Fred laughed out loud and applauded. The biggest surprise was the name of the bald one. He was the largest of the four, and he seemed to have a casual but solid self-confidence.

"Gino," I yelled at him, seeing how this was going. He nodded his head, and then I did the unthinkable in Japan. I hugged him. This was a huge faux pas in this culture, but he hugged me back, laughing. The real Gino, our road manager, and a man us Fools will never forget, had died a few years earlier so seeing a living honorarium was touching.

In no time we made our way to a stretch limo, which reminded me of how successful their late father had become. Juney kept up a steady patter along the way.

"We are going to have the best time! My father loved your band. You were his first job when he started at EMI, and he always spoke well of you. Every new album or CD that you put out, he would buy seven. He was a superstitious man and believed it would bring your band good luck. Your band still exists, so maybe it did."

He leaned forward and spoke to the driver. Then an endless compilation of Fools music filled the car for the next hour and half drive. The boys and Fred sang along with some of them, and talked loudly over others. It's an odd thing, but people often want to play your own music to you. I think I can speak for most musicians when I say that in social situations, I'd probably want to listen to something else. In this case though, it seemed to bring Shiggy's spirit back along for the ride.

Our destination was the Naeba Ski Resort, about a hundred miles from the airport. We weren't going there to ski, as it was summertime in Japan. We were going there for the Fuji Rock Festival, an annual three day event that brought some of the best bands in the world to Japan. Since 1997, bands and artists as diverse as Bob Dylan, Iggy Pop, Nine Inch Nails, Cold Play, The Cure, Gogal Bordello, The Beastie Boys, and Jonathan Richmond, to name a varied few, have played there.

The limo pulled into a luxury hotel about a mile from the festival entrance. Before we'd left America, Juney told me over the phone when I'd asked about accommodations, "just get here, my brothers and I will take care of everything else."

It was Friday, the first day of the festival, but the brothers had arranged a night of food, karaoke music, and toasts....many toasts.

"Freddy's shoes...*kanpai!*"

A very drunk but composed Gino gave that toast, and the bunch of us very drunk people all laughed and said "*kanpai!*" and tossed down another small glass of sake. *Kanpai* means 'dry cup' as if you are saying 'my cup is empty, who will fill it?' The toasts had started a bit solemnly a few hours before, happening in the midst of our wonderful meal.

It seemed the brothers had rented half the hotel, as the function room that we were in contained uncles, cousins, and wives. As the sake flowed, and some of the older or more temperate family members began to head off to their rooms, the toasts started to get silly as we moved into second, then third party (as the Japanese refer to it) toasts. The Japanese are a culture bound by many social protocols, but they party like they have three months to live. As you may look bad if you don't join in, I thought I was in my element but jeezus these people could drink.

We had already toasted the Fools, the Red Sox, the Patriots, Boston, Ipswich, and many other things that were obviously meant to honor me. Freddy, not a drinker, was delighted. I know you'll be shocked, but I was uncomfortable with the attention, and at some point I toasted the waiter who was serving us. They were all okay with that, and so when my turn next came around, I toasted a painting of Mount Fuji that was hanging on the wall. Juney, getting into the spirit, toasted the chandelier hanging above us. Richey then toasted Gino's bald head, to the falling down drunken laughing of the rest of us.

Though he wasn't drinking, Fred would yell 'kanpai' and laugh happily with the rest of us. He had resisted making a toast throughout the evening, always passing the honor on to me. Finally, after Stacey started a chant that went "num-ber seven, num-ber seven," Fred stood up and said this:

"Juney, Richey, Stacey, Gino, and your wonderful family and friends, I never had the honor of meeting your father but he must have been a quite a man."

The room got respectfully quiet as Fred continued, his new friends beaming at him. "I never thought I would get to know so many great people so quickly."

Juney nodded slowly as Fred spoke, smiling across at me. Fred had introduced the band for years, and he had a natural sense of timing. "I was trying to think of an appropriate toast, and I thought the simpler the better. So to honor all of my new friends," said Fred holding up an imaginary glass, "as they say in Italy, to your health, *CinCin!*"

There was an audible gasp in the room as the assembled guests looked at each other with wide eyes. Fred knew something was wrong, but he repeated his toast, imaginary glass still in his hand, "cin -cin...cin-cin!"

Gino, sitting next to me, said, "Why does he keep saying penis?" Fred nervously repeated the phrase one more time, but this time even louder, "CinCin!" He looked helplessly at me as the people in the room buzzed into a shocked undercurrent of conversation.

I stood up next to Fred and looked towards a puzzled Juney. "Juney, I was with him when the Italians said that. What's the matter?"

Fred slumped back down into his chair, confused and crestfallen.

Juney stood up and waited a moment until the room quieted down. "There has obviously been a misunderstanding here," he said. "I'm sure Fred didn't know that the word he's been repeatedly yelling means 'penis' in our language. He also seemed to be pantomiming holding one in his hand but as our friend Fred does not drink, he certainly meant that to be an imaginary glass. Fred we owe you an apology for ever thinking you would deliberately insult us."

With that, he bowed towards Fred and sat down.

The room was quiet for a moment, and then Richey started giggling, followed by Stacey, and then Gino, and soon the whole room was roaring in laughter. We laughed till we cried, and then laughed some more as sake followed more sake, each time with the loud toast of "CIN-CIN" and the imaginary penis in hand.

At some point the karaoke started. I remember singing a ridiculously drunken version of Gloria Gaynor's *'I Will Survive'* with Richey and Stacey. I remember hearing Fred sing *'Rock the Casbah'* and Gino sing *'Girls Just Want to Have Fun.'* It was a truly epic night, followed the next morning by a truly epic hangover, but it was worth every painful throb...we had bonded with Shiggy's family.

By Saturday afternoon we were all starting to feel human again, so we made our way onto the festival grounds by way of two golf carts the boys had somehow commandeered. They'd also procured VIP passes for all six of us, so we were granted prime viewing spots, and allowed entry to all of the back stage areas. There were three huge stages set up and over the course of a few hours, we saw Cold Play, Foo Fighters, New Order, and Los Lobos.

As we walked back stage later that night between band sets, I heard a voice yell, "Don't tell me they let fools in here!" I turned to see Doug Fieger, the lead singer of The Knack grinning at me. We'd opened for them on their first American tour in 1979. For six months they were the biggest band in the world, and yet in the midst of the *'My Sharona'* madness, they still gave us, the opening band, sound checks. I reminded him of that and he smiled and said, "of course."

By Monday morning, after a weekend of great music, great food, and a river of sake, Fred and I were back in the limo with the four brothers and headed for the airport. Within a year, Shiggy's boys would show up unannounced to see us Fools at The Hampton Beach Casino in New Hampshire, but on this day, we could be forgiven for thinking we'd never see them again.

As we piled out of the limo, the six of us stood there a bit uncomfortably, not quite knowing how to work this. It was Gino who took the lead. He gave Fred and me a funny look, and then gave us each a hug. The other three brothers followed suit. It was not only a gracious concession to an American custom, it also showed them to be part of a small but growing faction of young Japanese who were trying to break down certain age old customs.

Just before we turned away to head into the airport, Juney looked at Fred. He raised his hand as if holding an imaginary glass, or penis, and said, "Freddy, *cin-cin!*"

15

A Sparkle in the Forest

"There are things known and things unknown, and in between are the doors of perception."
Aldous Huxley

"I believe in a prolonged derangement of the senses in order to obtain the unknown."
Jim Morrison

(When thinking about how to approach this next chapter it occurred to me that I'm jumping all over the place, not only from location to location, but from time to time. For this I must beg the reader's indulgence and say that I'm telling the stories in the order that I remember them, and perhaps not always in the order in which they happened. I'm trying to place them in the relative context of what my band was doing at the time, because many of my adventures with Westlake seemed to happen during certain 'breaks in the action' of my musical career.

Whether Westlake planned it that way or it was just blind chance, I never thought to ask him. It could be that he was carefully choosing my time expeditions at periods when I was obviously available. That would certainly be in keeping with the meticulously planning man I knew.)

It was 1979, a few days after Christmas, and we Fools had just finished our first album for EMI and were enjoying a couple weeks off for the first time in over three years. The journey to that first album has been recounted in my previous book, but needless to say, it never would have happened had I not conquered my stage fright. Westlake's suggestion that I approach my shows as if I were a time traveler had allowed me over time, to see my position in front of the audience in a different non-threatening way, and to separate my anxiety from my performance. It was a revelation and it opened up a world of fun and energy to me. The audience had now become sacred to me.

It took some days to decompress. You see your bandmates pretty much daily for a few years and then you're back to the real world. Not to in any way diminish the much more important experiences of those in the armed forces, but in some ways it was like coming back from a tour of duty somewhere in the world. My Dad was a war hero who spent thirty-three months of World War II in North Africa and all over Europe, eventually fighting his way through France and into Germany, so I have great respect for the troops.

Initially it's almost a shock to be separated from your unit, or in my case, the band. But soon I was once again getting happily caught up with friends and family.

I hadn't seen Westlake in a while, and as always during these periods and even though I had ample evidence to the contrary, I would start to doubt my memories. The nature of the time travel experience was so other worldly that I would try and convince myself that it was a dream at best, or a self-creation at worst. Neither concoction played for long in my head, but I just mention it now to show how odd it was to try and walk in both worlds.

I'd been home for a couple of days when Gin told me, "We've been invited to a holiday party at the mansion."

Westlake never said as much, but I always felt sworn to secrecy about our travels. So how had I kept my secret time travel life from Gin? I did for a few years when we first got together, and then hinted at it, and then started to tell her the stories. For a while she treated the stories like it was an attempt on my part to entertain her but there was a day when her chin dropped and she took a deep breath.

"It's true! You asshole, why didn't you tell me it was?"

"I've been trying to," I said. "I guess I was trying to protect you from the craziness."

"Don't protect me anymore from that, and I'm going to need to know when and where you're going. I don't care if he says it's safe, I want you to run it by me first," she said.

I have ever since. Her take on the secrecy was this: "Who the hell would believe the story anyway?"

Initially our agreement was that we wouldn't let Westlake know that she's in on the deal, but my time traveling mentor was much too savvy not to pick up on Gin's inclusion in our secret. Later she became part of our planning.

So with that in our personal sails we drove up to the mansion for the holiday party. The place was decked out in lights and frills, to the point where even the stone lions out front each had on a party hat. Most of my family was in attendance; my Mom and Dad, my sisters Patti and Debbie, and my brother John. I hadn't seen them all together in such a long time and I was delighted to once again reconnect.

Some people over time lose the close knit feeling of their siblings surrounding them. I'm happy to say I never have. Aside from the many people I knew, there were countless other guests in attendance and it took us a while to make our way into the heart of the party.

I felt a tap on my shoulder and turned to see Hannah smiling at me. "Hi, Mike, hi, Gin! I'm so glad you two could make it," she said giving each of us a hug.

She and Gin had hit it off almost from their first meeting a few years earlier, to the point where they'd periodically gone out to lunch during my time away from home. They seemed to enjoy each other's company, and it was probably due, at least in part, to their similar personalities. They were both smart, loving, and caring...but if you crossed them, they would take you down. There was also the aspect that they both loved men who were away for long periods of time. I was thinking of how lucky Westlake and I were when he was suddenly at my side.

"Ah," he said smiling, "the prodigal son returns!"

There were more hugs and the kind of small talk friends make when they're catching up with each other. In some ways he looked the same age as I'd seen him when I was young, and yet now we seemed of a similar age. I asked him where his travels had taken him, but as always, he wanted to hear stories about a traveling rock band.

He and Hannah were soon pulled away in conversation with other friends, but just before that he leaned in and said quietly to me, "October 20, 1967. When you've researched that date, get back to me."

It was the odd start to another adventure, and one just as unlikely as any we'd undertaken. Not having any idea where we were going, I still felt a surge of excitement. It looked like I was once again going to skip into time.

****

Nowadays researching anything or anyone is as easy as picking up your smart-phone. Not only will your question be immediately answered, but there will be aspects of your search that open up other areas of information that you hadn't anticipated but in December of 1979, any research could only happen at your local library.

Thankfully, Ipswich had a wonderful old school library, but that didn't make my search any easier. October 20, 1967 was just a day in time, and at first I couldn't find anything that made it special. One thing about libraries though, they often contain librarians that are almost terminally bored and awaiting any chance to use their skills.

I met such a person. Eleanor Adler was attractive in the classic librarian way. She was stern, had her light hair in a bun, was tall and slender, and wore horned rim glasses. Her first reaction at seeing me seemed to be distaste. When I walked to her main desk area, she waited a minute before looking up, as if she really had more pressing business than dealing with a somewhat hairy human.

"Can I help you," she asked in the skeptical tone of someone who was quite sure she couldn't.

"I'm trying to find out about whatever might have happened on the day of October 20, 1967," is what I blurted out.

"May I ask why?" she asked, but I sensed a spark of interest.

"It's the day my daughter was born," I lied. "Someday I'd like to tell her what was going on when she came into the world."

In a blink I went from possible homeless weirdo to needy father, and Eleanor was on my team. The search only took an hour or so before we found what I was pretty confident Westlake had wanted me to find, but had I tried it alone, I doubt I would have succeeded.

Eleanor went through regional, and then national microfiche, viewing film of countless newspaper headlines from around the world for the day of October 20, 1967. There were headlines about war protests and civil rights trials. There were stories of unrest and riots in other countries. She tut tutted these items as if unfit for a father to tell a daughter. Then she came upon a story that seemed light and quirky enough to satisfy her idea of what I was trying to do.

"Here's an odd one," she said, "A couple of guys named Patterson and Gimlin claim to have filmed Bigfoot. It supposedly was taken in Bluff Creek, California on October 20, 1967."

BINGO!

I can't say how I knew that it was the story I was supposed to find, maybe it was just the outlier in all of the gloom and doom stories that took place on that date, but as I drove up the long hill the next day leading to the mansion, I was confident that I was right. And it was just like Westlake to test me prior to any excursion, making me toe some mark to prove my metal.

Hannah met me at the front door and said, "He's in the gym."

Westlake had converted one of the many downstairs rooms into a fully equipped training room, complete with weights, a stationary bike, and a small boxing ring. As I entered he was jumping rope and apparently had been for a while, judging by his sweaty appearance.

"Hey Mike," he said, skipping to a halt. "Are you still breathing?"

He wasn't asking me sarcastically if I was still alive, he was asking if I was still practicing the breathing technique he had taught me.

"Yes I am," I said. I wasn't lying either. I had learned a while back that while the purpose of Westlake's breathing exercises were for our travels through time, they also helped me control my breathing when I sang.

"Are you ready to run a bit?"

He slipped on a sweatshirt knowing my answer. Like most people I know, I was wearing sneakers so I was at least dressed for it. Westlake had gotten me into training mentality and physicality a few years before, and though I'd been slacking the last year or so, I felt I could still 'run a bit.'

"Let's do it," I said.

We ran off down the hill at a comfortable pace and headed left at the end of the long driveway towards a road that eventually led to the ocean.

"So Bigfoot, that's it right?" I asked after a half a mile.

"Good for you," he said, "I should give you harder tests."

With that we ran quietly on, which was good with me because after a mile or so, I was more dealing with breathing than talking. We turned back not long after, probably as much because Westlake wanted to talk, as him maybe wanting to save my overrun heavily breathing self. In my defense, I only said I could run 'a bit.' I was right.

"She looks real," I said. "The arms are so long, and she has no neck. When she turns her head, it's with her whole upper body. Why would someone think that was a good thing to fake? And why would someone who was making a costume decide to make a female to begin with? Why complicate the hoax?"

Westlake and I had watched the now famous Patterson-Gimlin fifty-three second film over and over and I was getting more convinced of its legitimacy. Westlake was non-committal, but his interest in the event spoke volumes.

I knew where it was going.

"So here's what I'm thinking," said Westlake. "You and I are mushroom hunters. That's the reason we will be in the Bluff Creek area. Mushroom hunting is a small but lucrative industry that goes well back into the fifties in northern California. I'm going to give you a quick study about mushrooms, but if we need to explain anything, let me do it."

I was once again ready to reprise my role as the quiet, but maybe slightly dangerous and deranged friend of the person everyone would be talking to. But so be it. I was about to go down the time pipe, so I was just happy to be along.

16

Of Lizard Kings & Hairy Queens

"A reasonable amount of danger is part of the price of living."
Louise Dickinson Rich

"But the truth was stranger than an aimless road. It always was."
Aspin Matis

"There are many millions of uninhabited acres out there, all over the world. If you were an intelligent hominid who wanted nothing to do with us homosapiens for whatever reason, there's lots of places in this world to hide. It's not a great leap to think that they would find humans to be threatening and alarming. Many of us humans feel the same way." Westlake was prepping me for our trip. He had a great way of playing both sides of a story. Moments earlier he was telling me about the many 'it's a man in a suit' theories that led some to believe it a hoax.

We were near the fountain in the back courtyard of the mansion. Alex and John had just brought the big wooden chair out. Looking at it, I felt the same mix of excitement and apprehension as I always did just prior to our time jumps. Westlake and I were dressed like northern California mushroom hunters, that is to say we looked like the kind of scruffy outdoors people you'd find in almost any recent era.

We were each equipped with a paring knife and an onion sack, and we both wore bright orange vests. The thinking was that if there were hunters in the area, we didn't want to look like prey. Westlake had given me a short primer on which mushrooms we were supposedly hunting, but I didn't pay much attention. If our survival came down to my mushroom knowledge, we were pretty much fucked.

"I'm going to get us there about an hour before the incident takes place. I recently investigated the area and determined that we should place ourselves on a low ridge that overlooks the dry wash bed where the sighting took place. It's also in the direction where the creature, if that's what it is, was walking. If it is a creature, it should walk right past where we will be hiding. If it's a person in a suit, I'm sure he or she won't stay in it for long after being filmed."

Hannah was sitting at the picnic table reading a newspaper, as if Westlake had just been talking about nothing more exciting than what color they would paint the spare bedroom. I wondered how many times she had sat there watching the man she loved blink out of sight, not knowing into what danger he might be headed. I suspected that by now she must have developed an anxiety saving disconnect.

I paused before sitting in the chair and just took in the moment. Hannah got up and gave Westlake a peck on the cheek. "See you soon," she said, "and maybe you'll bring me back some chanterelles."

It was one of the mushrooms we were supposedly hunting, much valued for its fruity but often spicy taste. Ok, I guess I did retain some mushroom knowledge. I then sat in the chair and we were off.

I was, as usual, bent over and trying to catch my breath but my first sensations were about the temperature (probably mid-seventies) and the smells (a rich deep forest mix of plants in either full bloom or full decay). Westlake tapped me on the back and I came into focus.

It's hard to explain what it's like to blink into another time. It's an instant alive feeling, as if your energy drink just kicked in. It might have something to do with the fact that you don't belong in that time place, and nature, or whatever rules the universe, is highlighting you as an intruder. Whatever the reason, I was wide awake.

We were in a deeply forested area but our landing spot was a small clearing on the ridge that Westlake had targeted. I looked forty yards down the slope to where, in the next hour or so, we were probably going to learn some things.

"This looks like a good place for chanterelles," Westlake said, as if that was the reason we were here.

He always amazed me with his ability to separate one moment from the next. I watched him dig about and find a few mushrooms, but I soon became fascinated by the sights and sounds and wandered back away from the ridge toward what sounded like a brook. I immediately realized how thirsty I was and walked towards the sound.

Then I saw him sitting there, legs folded in a lotus position next to a small running stream. He was a man I guessed to be in his middle twenties, of medium build, in jeans and a sweatshirt, and with what my Dad would have said was 'a good head of hair.' There was something about him that seemed familiar, but I couldn't quite place him.

He sensed my presence a moment after I saw him, but instead of acting surprised he put his index finger to his lips as if to shush me. His eyes then directed me to his right, and there, playing on the edge of the stream a few feet away from him was a small hairy human. I say human but more from the intelligence I sensed in him than in his actual looks, for he was distinctly not human.

He was about three feet high and, except for his face, the palms of his hands, and the soles of his feet, he was completely covered in a short brown hair. The top of his head, unlike a human's, was more crested than rounded, and he seemed not to have much of a neck. He was kneeling and watching a leaf float by, but it was when he stood up that I was most taken aback. Instead of a hunched over chimp like posture, he stood up straight. I could have almost believed it was a boy in some very well made costume, were it not for his unusually long arms, which hung nearly to his knees. I might have drawn a quick intake of breath, because he turned half around and saw me. He jumped back and with an almost human sounding yelp,, he bounded off into the bushes. I immediately noticed a very skunky smell hanging in the air.

"Damn," the man said standing up and giving me an odd wild eyed look while brushing off his pants. "So there are other strange two legged creatures in the forest."

It occurred to me that he might be either insane, or very high on something. I also couldn't get over the feeling that I'd seen him somewhere before. He

continued speaking, but as much to the woods around us as to me.

"He's only just learning how to do that. It's the same defense mechanism that skunks and honey badgers have. I was about to tell him you were here, and we might have avoided that stink, but then again it's good that he fears humans. Hell I fear humans. It might keep him from getting shot someday."

With that he stepped across the stream and gave me an appraising look, as if seeing me for the first time.

"I see you're not from around here," he said.

"You can talk to them," I stammered, "How did you....?" I ran out of words.

"I can talk to beings from other planets. I can make the Earth stop in its tracks. I can place myself anywhere in space or time. I am the Lizard King. I can do anything."

He said that last bit barely above a wild eyed whisper. It was at that moment that I recognized him.

"Hello, Jim," Westlake said coming up behind me. "What brings you to these far places? Is there a Doors show somewhere nearby?"

Yes, that Jim Morrison. The lead singer of the Doors. Jeezus.

"What brings me here? What brings me anywhere? I fill my hollow soul with experience. And right now I'm experiencing the bright orange vests you two are wearing and it's carving a hole in my brain. What possessed you two to walk in the woods dressed like fucking pumpkin people?"

I knew he was tripping as only someone who has done it could know.

"We're mushroom pickers and we dress this way so that hunters don't shoot us," Westlake replied.

"Well if I were you I'd worry about getting shot by pumpkin hunters," Morrison said.

I was having no luck trying to make sense out of that last statement, but he continued.

"Now if you'll pardon me, I've got to go find my little friend before his mom gets here. You pumpkins should go find a patch and hide somewhere. It would upset her to see you. It would upset anyone to see you. I'm starting to feel upset myself."

With that he stepped back across the stream and walked off in the direction his ' little friend' had taken. As he walked away he made odd little yips and chirps and at one point he voiced a low pitched chatter that could almost pass as a language. Listening carefully, I thought I heard a response. Westlake and I looked at each other.

"Ok, change in plans...let's go hide somewhere," he said.

We found a vantage point about fifty yards away in a small but thick copse of trees. Because of what just happened, we couldn't go back to our planned ridge overlook, but Westlake thought it was probably too late for that anyhow, and given what Morrison had said, 'mom' would be heading for this area to find her boy. While we waited, we removed our orange vests and put them in our onion sacks. We were now part of the foliage.

We saw her immense form walking, quietly towards the stream, but looking back over her shoulder as if to determine whether she was being followed. She had just encountered two brave fellows who'd been searching for her kind, one of them for a good part of his life. That same one had taken the film I'd seen countless times. She looked surprisingly unflustered considering what had just happened.

She must have been all of seven feet tall and had the wide heavy frame that I'd pretty much committed to memory. I was amazed that she could walk so quietly. Her very movement and nature spoke of intelligence as she neared the stream, but more so when she found no one there and started sniffing the air and grass. She became every bit the panicked Mom, spinning about and yipping and chattering, and looking off in the direction that her boy and babysitter had taken.

After a moment there was an answering yip and we saw the boy come running from a distance. He ran upright and at the last moment leapt into Mom's arms. There was the kind of reconnecting you'd have if you lost your kid in a mall. Not long behind the boy was Morrison, waving his arms and speaking in that chattering tongue we'd heard earlier. I had no doubt that he was tripping out of his skull, but Mom seemed to question him, he seemed to answer back, and all was good.

As we watched it all unfold from our hidey place, we knew our questions had been answered. Yes, the film was real, and yes, they are intelligent and live among us. As we were processing it all, we heard a low grunt from behind us. We turned and saw an enormous hairy man, but not a man, standing a few feet behind us. The fact that he could have got that close to us was stunning, more so because I was next to Westlake, and he didn't sense it either. Had we not seen the boy and Mom first, we might have totally freaked. Ok I'm speaking for me. I'd never seen Westlake freak.

I think of it now as us meeting Dad. I'm guessing he was about eight and half feet tall. He was all of Mom and more; a broad chest, powerful arms and legs, but the most startling thing was him looking at us with a direct and intelligent curiosity. It was totally disarming. His eyes seemed to decide that we were intelligent beings, and at that point, as if to ask 'what are you doing here?'...he left.

We sat there stunned for a moment. It had been a long day, but Westlake, ever the scientist, wanted to go investigate the original area that had been filmed. Patterson and Gimlin were long since gone on their endless hunt, but we were thrilled to visit the place we'd seen so many times on film.

As we stood there pondering all that had happened, we heard someone walking towards us through the woods. It was Morrison.

"Hey, Jim," Westlake said.

Morrison looked at us as if seeing us for the first time, and with wild eyes said, "If you're going up onto that ridge, just watch the fuck out. There are pumpkin people up there."

With that he walked off into the woods and we blinked back home.

17

Horsing Around

"*Nothing is so frustrating as arguing with someone who knows what he's talking about.*"
Sam Ewing

"*If everything seems to be going well you have obviously overlooked something.*"
Steven Wright

"I don't know how to make this work. We just got dumped by EMI after only two records. What do we do?"

I hadn't seen Westlake and Hannah in a while but even to my ears it sounded like I was whining. They were the first people, after Gin, I could talk to about it. It was 1981 and I was freaked out about being without 'a record company.' How does a band proceed?

"What do you want to do?" Westlake asked, ever the pragmatist.

Hannah seemed to be enjoying the back and forth, almost like she knew the outcome. She was only half listening though, as she was painting a landscape of the sloping field leading to the forest behind the house. It looked like it was going to be quite good.

"I want to keep playing," I said.

"Then do it," Westlake said. "Did you start playing because you really wanted a record contract or because you really like playing music?"

It was a rhetorical question. I couldn't think of a rhetorical answer.

"Trust me," he said, this break with EMI will be the best thing that ever happened to you."

A few years later, when I realized how right he was, I would think back on the conversation and wonder if Westlake had gone ahead a few years and taken a peek. After all, he never said he didn't go into the future. He said he didn't like to. (For more on this part of Fools history, read that book I've already mentioned numerous times.)

"I know just the thing to get you out of your self-pitying. There's a place I want to travel to, and I'd like you to come along."

That was how he spoke about time travel; it was never 'there's a time I want to travel to,' it was 'there's a place I want to travel to.'

"But first during this down time before you get your musical career back on track, you'll need to spend the next month getting back to your training. Do your running, your breathing, and your meditating, and stop shaving. Your hair length is fine.

And I want you to spend at least a few days each week riding one of my horses. Not the same one every day, mix them up. You were starting to get good at it a couple years ago, but you'll have to get better in a short time. Not just trotting this time, challenge yourself. I've set up a course around the property. It's about a mile long and some of it's a bit rough. Time yourself and try to get faster each time. And when you finish with the horse each day, don't leave him for the stable boy to put away. You'll put the saddle away, muck out his stall, brush him down, and feed and water him. I want you to do all of this as if your life depends on your skill and his happiness.

I've also had a small rifle range set up in the cellar, so we'll get to practice with a weapon accurate to the time period. And one more thing, get to the library and investigate The Corps of Discovery."

As I rode home to Gin, I realized my mood had changed from a confused depression to an almost light hearted sense of purpose. The Corps of Discovery sounded vaguely familiar, but I couldn't recall from where or when. But no matter, we were once again going to jump into time.

Crack! Boom! It was my first time shooting a muzzle loader. There was a target not far away that I winged, but the kickback on my shoulder was what impressed me. I'd followed Westlake's instructions about the prepping and loading of the gun, and all I could think was that if I needed to shoot it quickly, I was screwed.

"The important thing is to not put in too much powder. Fill that tip of the hollow antler to about the halfway point and pore it in. Then the paper wad, and ball, and use the ram rod to jam it to the bottom. I have no plan for using these guns, but we need to know how to pass for locals, so keep doing this till it is second nature."

So I loaded and fired the flintlock countless times and wondered how much Westlake had paid for such accurate recreations. As hard a find would probably be the appropriate monies and every day odds and ends, but then he was a very rich man, and he could make things happen.

Pretty much every even casual student of American history knows about the Lewis and Clark expedition, but fewer know it by its real name: The Corps of Discovery. It was then President Thomas Jefferson who in 1804 contracted Merriweather Lewis and William Clark to head up a mission of exploration into the newly acquired Louisiana Purchase, nearly a million square miles of territory.

The mission had two main objectives, to initiate trade and sovereignty over the Native American tribes along the Missouri river, and secondly, to find a practical route to the Pacific Ocean, a 'northwest passage.' It was hoped that much, if not all, of the journey could be made by boat, which really shows how little was known about the land west of St. Louis.

The two leaders were accompanied by thirty-one handpicked adventurers, many of them current or former military.

"Ok, we'll be leaving in about a week," said Westlake a few weeks after I began prepping. "I've just got to procure a few more things. I've got a Hollywood prop company working on our outfits. They've scoured museums looking at old paintings and recreations of clothing appropriate to 1804. We will be gold prospectors. While prospecting that far west is unusual for 1804, I doubt we can pass for hunters, or anything else pertinent to the time and area. Besides, a gold rush started two years earlier in North Carolina, so we won't seem anything worse than eccentric. Also, we may be spending a few days away, but I think you're ready for it. We'll be nothing more than exhausted when we get back.

I thought about that. On our previous trips, Westlake was able to return us not long after our departure, though we'd been gone for many hours. He said that he occasionally picked a later time in the returning day if he knew that Hannah had things to do away from the mansion. That's how casual these two had become about something I still saw as miraculous.

"Lewis, much more than Clark, is an educated man, so I will talk of my Harvard education. You will be my quiet nephew, but I encourage you to study the idioms and quirks of the spoken English of that time period. And when we get there, listen carefully to how people speak. One more thing, stop bathing. We can't show up smelling like flowers."

"I'm not sure I can explain that one to Gin," I replied.

Westlake looked at me and half-smiled. "Does she know about our trips?"

I looked away and shrugged. "Maybe," I said..

He nodded. "I knew that eventually you'd have to share it with her."

"Are you angry?"

"Of course not. She is your partner and if you trust her with the secret, it's okay. Besides, who would believe these things we do."

I laughed because that was exactly what Gin and I had thought for a while.

"So tell Gin that, even though we are carrying muskets, we will be safe. Throughout the twenty-eight months and almost eight thousand miles to the Pacific and back, the Corps only lost one man, and that was to appendicitis."

The fact that Westlake suspected that Gin was now in the loop shouldn't have surprised me, as her and Hannah had become good friends.

"You still haven't told me where or why we're going," I said, changing the subject.

"The date is May 25, 1804. We're going to a small village on the Missouri called La Charrette. By the time we get there our horses and supplies will have arrived from St. Louis, That's something I will have arranged a few days earlier on a separate trip."

"You're going twice?"

"Yes. This one will take more logistics than our normal trips. The 'why' we're going is a bit more complicated. Jefferson instructed Lewis and Clark to make daily entries in their journals, cataloging anything and everything they encountered. They were to make maps, collect plants, document encounters with the tribes and draw pictures of strange beasts.

Over the course of the trip they wrote over a million words, and were the first white men to see something as mundane as a prairie dog, and ferocious as a grizzly. Oddly though, there was a period where for a few months Lewis stopped writing. It's never been properly explained, and the most common school of thought leans towards a 'lost journal' that would cover the time period.

But recently I recovered a letter written many years later from Clark to a relative. In it he discusses his friend's death by suicide in 1809, and says something quite curious. Clark wrote 'he was sorely troubled by something he saw at Charrette. When he described it to me I said it be best to omit such a spectacle from our journals, lest we be perceived madmen. I now regret my reluctance. It made him doubt his own sanity, and for a time he would put no pen to paper.'"

"Jeezus," I said. "What the hell did he see?"

"That's what we hope to find out. Now it might be best if you lay low from your friends, family, and bandmates for a few days til we leave. They might think that from the smell, the EMI breakup has overly affected you."

So I went into pre travel mode again, and as usual, I was in equal parts excited and apprehensive. But such is the life of a foolish time traveler.

18

Strange Days

"Not all those who are lost are wandering, some are really lost."
Unknown

"The universe is not only stranger than we suppose, but stranger than we can suppose."
JBS Haldane

"Damn, but this shit is starting to feel comfortable, although it is a bit heavy for this time of year," I said, standing near the fountain behind the mansion.

The chair was in place and ready for us. I was wearing the same leather clothes and moccasins I'd been wearing around the clock for the last week, as per Westlake's orders.

The thinking was that we needed to look like we lived in them, which is what frontiersmen of that time period did when they were on the move. I had to avoid being seen by friends, or worse to be smelled by them, so I'd been living at the mansion.

We both had the aroma of long dead rats, so much so that Hannah had a couple of tents set up in the yard for us, and it was there we slept, lest we bring our stink into the building.

"I know it's been a tough week, but it should give you more respect for what those people went through. But when we get there, the weather should be warm enough that you can take off your top coat. The leather pullover hunting jersey is pretty comfortable."

W
estlake had spent god knows what on having exact replicas of frontier clothing made, and though I

complained about the warmth, I had begun to realize the practicality of the outfit; it was warm on cool nights and nearly waterproof.

Also the buffalo hide overcoat was thick enough to at least blunt, if not repel an arrow attack, though our chances of encountering any hostile activity were pretty slim.

Except for an isolated incident, the Native Americans the Corps encountered were more interested in trade, or in receiving the gifts of beads and tobacco that Lewis and Clark were known to be handing out. Both of us also wore furry hats, mine of coonskin, and his of fox. With our rifles in hand, we looked like the same kind of wild, hairy mannequins we'd seen portrayed in the dioramas at the Peabody Museum at Harvard.

We walked over to the chair and saw Gin and Hannah standing about ten feet away. Normally this would be 'peck on the cheek' time, but such was our condition that neither woman came closer.

"Good luck," Hannah said as Gin gave me a wave.

"See you in a while," said Westlake.

And with that, I sat in the chair, he stood behind it, and we were off.

My first reaction after catching my breath was to marvel at how clean and crisp the air felt. My second reaction was holy shit; I'm back in the nineteenth century! After all, this was the first time we'd jumped back to a time period where even my Dad wasn't yet alive. Our previous trips had been amazing, but it just sunk in that I was about to experience a time period way outside of my own.

We were in a small clearing, and I could hear the sound of a river nearby. As always on these trips, I felt amazingly alive. It's perhaps the result of wandering into another timeline that puts the body on total alert so that the senses are all heightened. It's nothing you are doing deliberately, but whatever the cause, it's exhilarating.

Much like Spinal Tap guitar player Nigel Tufnell, your personal amp 'goes up to eleven.' It's probably this high level of expended energy that ultimately leads to the exhaustion you feel upon your return.

Westlake seemed to be getting his bearings and after a moment he said, "It's about six in the evening, look around for some dry wood. It'll be a chilly night."

We gathered and stacked dry twigs and branches for the next hour. We then loaded our rifles, and as I followed Westlake, we made our way towards the sound of the river. It was an average looking river, not that fast flowing, and not very wide. I didn't know it at the time, but the mighty Missouri that this river flowed into was only a few miles away.

"Ah, there he is," Westlake said, looking a ways down the river to an area, almost like a beach, where a man dressed like us was waiting with five horses, two of them loaded with supplies. We made our way down to him and I immediately saw suspicion in his eyes.

"Hello Regis," Westlake said to him. "*Comment vas-tu, mom ami?*"

I saw the man relax somewhat as Westlake whacked him on the shoulder. He was a man I guessed to be in his late twenties, but there was a world of experience in his demeanor.

"I don't know what to think of you, Patrice," he said. "You come and go like a dream. I won't ask how you get to this place without a horse or canoe, because the tobacco you bring me is unlike any other and your coin is also good. But someday we will drink on that and you will tell me your secrets."

"Someday, my friend," Westlake replied.

"Now who is this one with you?" Regis asked looking hard at me.

Westlake bowed slightly and said, "Regis Loisel, allow me to introduce to you my nephew and friend, Michael Girard."

"It is a pleasure, Michael," Regis said as we shook hands and eyed each other.

"The pleasure is mine," I replied.

I decided he was a good dude. I think he decided the same about me, because he took a breath and smiled at both of us.

Westlake searched a pack horse and pulled out a bottle of something strong. We found a place to sit and pass it around. After a bit of small talk, much of it in French, Westlake said this to our new friend:

"So I know they camped here today, and I know you are trading with the expedition. What are your thoughts about the leaders?"

Regis was holding the bottle. He took a pull, and handed it to me.

"They are both strong men," he said, "but them coming through with so many gifts will change this area. I don't know if this is good. Most trappers have spent years building relationships with the Sioux. Now these men come here and will buy their way into the chief's teepee. Some trappers will be angry, but me, I see opportunities."

"You strike me as a smart man," I said to Regis.

Westlake gave me a bit of side eye, reminding me to limit what I said.

"Thank you, *Mon ami*," Regis replied. "As to the men, Clark is strong and practical but he will spend a day to make a decision about which hand to use to scratch his ass. Lewis is strong and impractical. If his hands were busy, he would try to use his foot to scratch his ass. A couple days ago, he almost fell off a cliff because he needed to see things from above. I'm told that Clark was not happy about that. But, ass scratching techniques aside, their men trust them, and whether this intrusion is good or not, I trust them too."

We sat near the river for some moments in silence. And then Regis broke it.

"You puzzle me, Patrice. I feel you are a long lost brother, but from no mother I can place. You seem to know me and my business, but we have no mutual friends. My mind tells me there is something not right. But my stomach tells me you are to be trusted. I will trust my stomach."

Westlake barked out a laugh and said, "Someday my friend I will tell you things that you will have a hard time believing. But for now, what is happening today at the camp? And will you introduce us to the captains?"

Regis rubbed his hairy chin for a moment before replying. "It's a poor village. There might be six French families here. There is not much for the expedition to do but rest up for tomorrow. They want to leave early in the morning but yes I will introduce you. And what shall I tell them you do?"

"We are gold prospectors," Westlake replied. "And we are scouting out new areas of opportunity."

Regis squinted his eyes in disbelief and laughed.

"Well you will have the entire business to yourselves as there are no gold prospectors east of Virginia," he said.

"There will be," Westlake replied. Regis paused and looked at Westlake carefully and said this:

"I will introduce you on the condition that you alert me, prior to anyone else, about your gold discoveries. " Regis was a quick fellow.

"Done," Westlake said, spitting on his hand and offering it to Regis, who spit on his. The two shook hands.

"Come in the morning, early," Regis said, and with that he climbed onto a horse and trotted off towards the tiny village of La Charrette, about a mile up the river.

Westlake nodded at me in satisfaction.

"Will you go back and tell him about where he can find gold?" I asked.

Westlake thought a moment and said, "Yes."

Westlake and I brought the four horses with us back to the clearing, made a fire and set up camp. It was my task to work up a meal, something my friends and family would rightfully tell you would sorely test my skills.

Prior to our trip, I was told to research just such a situation, and I was eager to give it a try. Once again

Westlake had done his homework, as I found some hard tack in our supplies. It's a simple biscuit whose history goes back to Roman times; made of flour, water, and salt. The trick is that once it's cooked over low heat three or four times to remove the moisture, it's then a viable food source for months to come.

Using the handle of my knife, I broke the rock hard stuff into pieces and placed it into a small pan. I then added some water and some pemmican. The latter is a paste of dried and pounded meat mixed with melted fat and other stuff that was a staple of the North American tribes...think beef jerky. To my great surprise and delight, after a few minutes of cooking, the mixture was not only edible, but pretty friggin tasty! Westlake even liked it. Take that Bobby Flay!

We sat for a while looking at the stars. With no city lights or pollution, they were magnificent. Westlake began to speak.

"We have a big morning tomorrow. We can't seem too important or we will change the time line. If that happens we won't learn what we came to find out. Follow my lead, and don't talk too much."

Once again I was tasked with something I don't do well...being quiet, but I went to sleep thinking of being onstage and babbling to an audience during a Fools show on some tour somewhere.

Oh the irony.

19

When the Still Seas Conspire

"Never annoy an armed man."
Kelley Armstrong

"I may not have gone where I intended to go, but I think I ended up where I needed to be."
Douglas Adams

It rained during the night and our lean-to was hard pressed to keep out the rain, so when first light came we were glad to be up. We packed our stuff, ate some food and were off. It was an easy ride to the tiny settlement, but it allowed me time to tamp down my feelings of wonder. We heard the sounds of activity not long before we saw the place. It was a simple six shack town, built near the river.

There were men busy everywhere getting the three boats ready, the main boat being the keel boat, about fifty feet long. We spied Regis talking to a man who seemed to be in charge of those loading and boarding the boats. We dismounted and walked through the busy scene and came face to face with Captain William Clark.

Meeting people you've read about in history books will test your composure; you know their major life events, their successes and failures, and in some cases you know the date and cause of their death. I've said it before, but in a way, it makes them sacred. It was hard not to look at these people with wonder and pity, but I was able to walk back my emotions and handle the moment.

Clark gave us a curious glance. "What have we here?"

He was about Westlake's height, a little over six feet, and had the look of a no nonsense leader of men.

Regis stepped between us and introduced us to Clark as his gold prospecting friends, recently from Virginia.

Clark gave us a slight bow and said, "I'd of thought there's enough gold in Virginia to keep your kind from venturing this far west. But I would caution you, the Indians in this area are mostly friendly and interested in trade. But a few days north you will encounter the Sioux, and if they perceive the slightest weakness in either you or your young friend, they will try and take whatever they want from you...your supplies, your horses, even your lives. If you are to continue, I would advise you to tread carefully."

With that, he turned back to his work. We had been inspected, advised, and dismissed. It irritated me that while I was called the 'young friend,' in reality both Lewis and Clark were roughly my same age, but I must say that I took them to be older. As it played out in history, the life expectancy for most males at that time in America was about forty, so in their own way, they were older. When I commented on our short moment with Clark, Westlake told me that our encounter had gone perfectly.

"We only wanted to meet him, not make a lasting impression," he said.

We turned away from Clark and followed Regis through the crowd to a man sitting at a small portable writing table. He seemed oblivious not only to us but to all that was going on around him, and he wrote in a quick, sure hand. Regis bent down and spoke quietly to Captain Merriweather Lewis, who stood up and stretched.

"Anything to get away from this infernal task," he said to no one in particular.

Like Clark, he was taller than most of his men, and also like Clark he had an air of strength and command about him. But unlike Clark, he didn't try to hide his contempt for our supposed prospecting venture.

"What ridiculous nonsense! Are you both insane? Do you think I bring nearly forty well-armed and well trained men to this wilderness for show? There are a hundred ways that even careful men could die out here!"

I sympathized with his take on us; here he was at the last tiny outpost of white people he would see in some thousands of miles, heading into possibly years of unknown danger, and he encounters, in his mind, two oblivious nitwit gold hunting greenhorns.

He looked at me dismissively and then said to Westlake, "you sir, look like a man who can handle himself, but what good will come of you bringing the ingénue?"

It was the second time in a few moments that I had been called a child and I bristled. I looked hard at Lewis and blurted out.

"I could outshoot you in a heartbeat."

I didn't mean to say it, and I didn't even mean that it might be true, it just came out. I heard Westlake make a sharp intake of breath, or maybe it was mine, but I knew I'd made a misstep.

Our task once again was to meet and interact, but not to make a deep impression, so as not to change the timeline, that we might get an accurate view of what we came to see. Lewis looked surprised at not only my comment, but that I had made one. He smiled.

"Well then, we could all use an occasional distraction. Let's walk out back and find a target," he said, picking up his musket and leading us behind the shack.

You'd think that someone who had read about Lewis, like I had, would know enough not to challenge him to a shooting match. The man had been not only a hunter, but a sharp shooter since he was barely a teen. Yeah, you'd think that, but there we were walking out back to a shooting match.

Westlake, rather than being upset, seemed amused and resigned and as we walked he said simply, "Breathe and hold." It was what he'd said to me countless times just before I fired the musket I was now holding.

As we walked the short distance we were joined by many and soon most of the frontiersmen. It seemed that the entire tiny town and its visitors were assembled for our impromptu contest. It was obviously an entertainment starved town, but some stupid part of me liked the attention...I would have an audience. In the past it would have tortured me to have this many watching, but now it was at least something I was at home with for better or worse.

Lewis stopped at a spot which surveyed a wide marshy expanse and pointed.

"Pick some target, and if you hit it, I will pick some farther target or concede."

Thinking back, I was most impressed with his lack of arrogance toward a nitwit like me. To him, it was simply a shoot off.

I've played pool with the dickhead types who try to give you the 'stink eye' look before your possible game winning shot on the eight ball. Not Lewis; although he obviously saw me as a lightweight, he gave me no such look. He was ready for a contest, and happy if I could give him one.

We must now talk about my weapon, because while it looked exactly like the muskets of the day, it was crafted to another level. The concept of 'rifling' or spiraling a groove inside a gun barrel to make the projectile spin, and stay more accurately on an intended line was not new to 1804 but by the twentieth century it had become an art form.

Adding to that was the fact that my musket balls had no seam in them. Yes, they were lead made and poured into tiny cups but back then they weren't spun to eliminate the tiny equator line that the old musket balls lived with.

To say I had an advantage would be an understatement, but I was young, stupid, and pissed off at being dissed by a hero of mine who had been dead a hundred and seventy years before I met him. Spin your head around that.

Lewis waited patiently while I surveyed the landscape. I was one part freaking out and one part still pissed off, and a further part wondering why the hell I'd never learned to shut the fuck up!

I looked across the marsh and spied a broken tree about a hundred and fifty yards away. Whether by lightning or storm, it had a 'v' shape to it. Each limb of the 'v' stood up about a foot. By any standard, it would be an almost impossible shot. But if we both missed, maybe my challenge would be forgotten.

I pointed it out. "The broken branch on the left."

I dropped to a knee to get in my ready to shoot mode. I was no longer mad at Lewis for dissing me, I just didn't want to look like a dope who didn't belong. I cocked the gun, and went through the ritual Westlake had taught me. Sight the target, breathe, and hold. I pulled the trigger and looked thru the smoke to see that I'd winged the target; a part of the broken branch on the left was no longer there.

There were immediately yells of wonder and support from the assembled watchers. It was a pretty good shot. As I stood up Lewis looked at me with some surprise, and laughed.

"I can match that shot but I don't think I can better it," he said. "I misjudged you. Well done, sir."

He then nodded, shook my hand and prepared to head back to the boats. Clark was now also in attendance. There was a grumbling among the assembled that Lewis quickly picked up on. He was their guy, would be not also shoot?

He sighed, raised his rifle, and under his breath he said to me, "the one on the right."

His gun fired and the other side of the 'v' branch exploded. His men cheered their approval. While they were still talking about his first shot he was reloading. When he finished doing that, still standing, he winked at me and said, so that only I could hear, "I'll get the rest of yours."

And then once again standing, not kneeling like I was, and using a weapon that he didn't know was ancient and impossibly inaccurate...and with all his men and Clark watching, he shot away the rest of the branch that I'd hit part of. His people went nuts. It was the most amazing and casual act of not only marksmanship, but showmanship that you could possibly join together.

I looked at Westlake and saw that, like me, he was shaking his head in disbelief.

Lewis, unfazed by the noise and adoration of his troops, looked at me and said," I could use a shooter like you."

We all walked back to the small dock and within moments the keel boat and the two long canoes were ready to depart. Lewis before boarding, turned to Westlake and I.

"I hope you two will reconsider. You're good men, but I'm not sure you understand what awaits you. But maybe none of us do. Keep your guns loaded and your eyes open."

He turned and made his way onto the keel boat. Regis held back a moment and said to me, "thanks for giving us all a display. It allowed the Captain to show his grit. The men were encouraged."

Then to Westlake he said, "I don't know your intentions. Mine are that I will go up the river with them, and introduce them to the Sioux chief who waits three days forward. There is a trail not far off the river that follows it north. Perhaps I will see you somewhere but be mindful that there are rumors of a powerful medicine man somewhere in this area, and that there might be Sioux warriors in the neighborhood for that reason."

He nodded at us and got aboard the keel. All three boats were soon out of sight.

My first thought was to apologize to Westlake. "I fucked up when I challenged him. I'm sorry, I got carried away in the moment. I can't seem to separate myself from the time like you do. I'll understand if you no longer want me along."

Westlake smiled and put his hand on my shoulder.

"Stop! That was the best thing I've seen in years. Your shot was great and because of that we got to see a frontier legend in action. It was amazing. No matter how it all goes down, that was worth the trip. Now we will follow the boats along the shore and see what ensues."

So we climbed onto our horses and made our way north by way of a trail along the river. We rode along in a comfortable silence, enjoying the improving weather, and the wonderful sounds of the river and the old growth forest around us. Some of these trees had trunks that would have taken five large men holding hands to encompass them; that's if you could find five large men to hold hands. Some of the trees were easily over two hundred feet tall.

This was America before the European Invasion. It wasn't quite a Garden of Eden, but nature wise, it must have been close. It teamed with wild fruit and vegetable edibles, and a vast array of game. When animals abound, some of them will be predators...and of those predators, the most fierce and dangerous is a two legged man. Ok, I reread that and even I wondered about the phrasing. Am I implying that there are three or even four legged men? Let's move on.

We rode along and towards midday we could once again hear, but not see, the boats apparently not too far west of us.

Since the Corps was going up river, the good part of the work was done with rowing, much of it hard. And as areas became difficult, for whatever reason, they would go ashore. The long canoes they could carry, but the fifty foot keel boat would have to be pulled up the river by men on the banks.

During rough stretches it was not uncommon for the expedition to make only five miles a day. On the return trip many months later, and coming down the Missouri with the current, they often made seventy miles a day.

"So what are we looking for?" I asked Westlake as we rode along.

"We don't know what we're looking for. What we do know is that Lewis stopped writing for an extended period around this time. We just watched him this morning writing at that small table near the dock. He complained about it, but he did it nonetheless. There must be some other part of this story."

We rode on in silence and the day passed. By late afternoon we were looking for a place to set up camp. We found a clearing not far off the trail and the river. It was Westlake who first heard the far off commotion. It sounded to my ears like hearing a band outside from far away. All you could hear were the drums. We climbed back onto our horses and rode towards the noise and after about a half a mile, we crested a ridge and looked down on a scene. By now we could also hear the singing as we watched warriors dancing and leaping as they circled some others who were playing drums. But there was someone in the center near the drummers dancing wildly to his own vision. He was long haired, shirtless and painted, and as we got closer, I realized that he was screaming in English.

"The dead are walking with no limbs and wild lights! The night seas are boundless and filled with renegade dreams!"

The warriors bounced and danced in delirium as the wild man raved on.

"These are the wilderness children! They are slaves to freedom and naked realms. Behold their madness!"

As we got closer, the wild man's voice rang a familiar tone. I could also see the telltale sparkle around him.

"Who will forgive us for wasting this sunset!?" the man bellowed. "The souls pile upon each other in endless glee! Load your guns with gin and blossoms for I am the Lizard King!"

He bellowed this last bit as I saw him for who he was. It was Jim Fucking Morrison...again.

"What the fuck is he doing here?" I asked. "Is he a traveler?"

"Yes," Westlake replied.

"Is he following us?"

Westlake looked stunned. It was the first time I'd ever seen him confused, even for a moment.

"No, I don't think so. In both places he was there before us, and we found him. There something strange about all of this. He must know some things about time travel that I don't."

"Patrice! Michael! We meet again!" said Regis coming up behind us astride a painted pony.

Riding next to him on a much larger mount was Lewis. He nodded to us.

"I see you found the Sun Talker," Regis said. "I heard he was here so I brought the Captain to see him."

"You didn't tell me he was a white man, Regis," Lewis said looking down on the spectacle. Morrison was now dancing wildly among the braves, who seemed in awe of him.

"Yes, a white man," Regis said. "A crazy white man. The Indians revere him as a holy man. They say he can make miracles. I've tried to talk to him but he speaks crazy things and doesn't seem to see me."

"Do you know how long he's been here?" Westlake asked.

"I think perhaps six weeks if I understood the chief correctly," Regis responded.

Westlake and I looked at each other. Morrison had been here for six weeks? That was stunning to us. Westlake had once stayed away for over a week and paid a physical price for it. To visit a time line for six weeks was unheard of to us.

"Something's happening," Regis said.

The scene below had quieted. Morrison had stopped dancing, and the drums had come to a sudden halt. Morrison had his arms extended as if he were a predator ready to claw the air, and he seemed to hear something. His head tilted, as if he was sniffing the wind. He seemed to see all of the braves in front of him for the first time. We were close enough to see pity in his eyes. Then the almost dark sunset sky brightened in a curious way. Morrison seeing this, again went wild man.

"The defilers have returned!" Morrison screamed. "Run my brothers! They will have us if we stay! We have no way to thwart them! Be gone and run with me!"

He ran full off through the woods and the braves followed him at his considerable speed. Except for one older brave who probably knew he could not keep up with the younger ones. He paused to look up at the changing sky as an odd thing happened.

A bright disc appeared out of the mist and slowly descended above the old man. We watched in awe as it hovered twenty feet above him, and then a beam locked onto the stunned old man and started to lift his terrified self through the air into the disc. He twisted and fought as he was slowly lifted upward. Lewis, among us on the hill, was the only one not frozen by the creepy sight.

"I will not have it!" he yelled, and drawing his sword, he raced his horse down the hill at full speed toward the disc.

We all bolted after him, Westlake drawing the archaic pistol from his belt. The disc seemed to sense our threat and slowly slide across the field, the old man suspended below. Lewis reached it first and swung his sword through the beam, just above the suspended man. The disc hesitated just as Westlake fired his pistol at it. If he hit it, it made no noise, but the old man dropped to the ground. The disc wobbled twenty feet above us, and then blinked out of existence. Regis jumped off of his horse and got the very confused and terrified old man back on his feet. The rest of us, horses and men breathing heavily, were still unable to speak.

"What fucking curse was that?" Lewis asked Westlake.

Westlake gathered himself and said truthfully, to my surprise, "I've heard of this, but I've never seen it. You saved him. Well done, sir."

Lewis shook off the compliment, as if it was something anyone would have done. It wasn't.

We rode through the woods, the old man riding up behind Westlake until we found the braves, who were delighted to see him, but otherwise seemed to be in a state of mourning. Morrison was nowhere to be seen. Regis talked to them. He was told that Sun Talker had brought them to safety, and then disappeared. The old man bowed his thanks at Lewis and handed him a strand of beads. Lewis bowed in acknowledgement of the gift...and we rode off.

Lewis had apparently had enough for one night. He appeared visibly shaken, and it was obvious that it took much to do so.

"I have no way to place that thing in my records," he said. "If I tell Clark this, he will think me mad. I know you would vouch safe my story, but to what end? I will think on this, but I see no way to bring it to reason. I thought our voyage would bring surprises but nothing like this wild madness. Thank you, Patrice and Michael. Whatever worse might have happened tonight was avoided with your help. Fare you well. Regis, let us return."

We watched them ride off into the night. There were so many questions, but we wouldn't answer them tonight. Westlake got off his horse, so I got off of mine.

"Well that was quite a trip," he said and a moment later we blinked out of time and place and were back to the mansion; it was just another day in eternity.

20

Weird Scenes Inside the Goldmine

"There is an electric fire in human nature tending to purity"
John Keats

"Life is hard. It's harder if you're stupid."
John Wayne

"So is that why Lewis probably stopped writing? I mean it had to be a shock for him to encounter a UFO," Hannah said.

We were sitting at the table in front of the fountain. We'd been back for a couple of hours, had both showered and as we were starting to feel human again, told our story to Gin and Hannah.

"I think someone from our time period would be better prepared for it, just because UFO stories have been part of our culture for years," Gin said. "Even Mike saw one. But I can't imagine someone from 1804 seeing one."

(Yes friends...even Mike saw one as a teen. His younger brother John was there at his side. And it may have been a close encounter but that's a story for another day.)

"Well someone from 1804 did see one," Westlake said. "For all we know, it was just another sane man seeing something that tested his reason. Because of that it went unreported."

"I think it's apparent that someone of Lewis' character and courage would have been seriously scrambled by what you all saw," Hannah said.

"A man who religiously recorded every unusual plant and animal he saw, felt unable to report on such a stunning 'fucking curse' as he called it," I added.

"He must have carried that with him for the rest of his life. I know we've talked about Lewis and his reaction, but we seem to be taking the flying saucer for granted. What are you thinking Mike?" Westlake said.

He was right. For some reason my thoughts were about Lewis' heroism, and not the strange occurrence that had brought it about. And even that incredible moment was overshadowed by a bigger question.

"The saucer thing freaked me out," I said. "It brought back stories we've all heard of abductions, and even cattle mutilation. But some part of me always thought it was real, so I guess that's why I, in some way, took that for granted. But to me, the story is Morrison. How the fuck was he back there for six weeks? You always said the longest you ever stayed was a week and that it wiped you out. "

We were all quiet for a bit thinking of the concept of a rock star freely traveling through time and not a small (r) rock star like me. I mean an honest to god, still hear his name in a hundred years ROCK STAR! Jim Fucking Morrison. He was traveling through time and staying for extended periods, and he was obviously tripping his brains out while he was doing it.

It was a puzzle unlike any others. For us to discover that Bigfoot was real, or to discover why Lewis stopped writing his journals...these were questions that puzzled even the most casual delvers into history. But other than us, no one was wondering how Jim Morrison was traveling thru time, or how he was able to do it so well.

"We need to investigate this, Mike," Westlake said. "As much as to try and solve the mystery as to add to our own travel knowledge. Find us a Doors show to visit, and maybe we'll get to ask him some questions. This time we won't care if we interfere with a time line. You can even challenge him to a scream off if you'd like."

That was Westlake being funny.

****

Jim Morrison was a strange dude. He was probably more, in his mind, a poet than a rock singer, but his pursuit of the two, added to his wild and colorful personality, and his strong voice, made him one of the most iconic front men in rock n' roll history.

He was known for giving powerful but erratic performances, sometimes leaving the stage for long periods, and at other times reciting his poetry, or ranting about whatever political thing was on his mind in the middle of any given song. Though it's now hard to believe, the early reviews of Doors shows, before they hit, speak of Morrison as keeping his back to the audience, and making people feel uncomfortable. This may just have been him finding his place, or maybe like many showbiz types, it could have been him dealing with stage fright.

In any event, whatever powered him soon made him and his band a must see experience. There were shows that he left early, there were more than a few shows where he collapsed, leaving some to wonder if it was part of the show.

It likely wasn't. He was a heavy user of whatever he could drink, sniff, or swallow, and he apparently did not separate work from pleasure. From all these years later it looks increasingly like he might have been one of the more unhappy rock stars ever.

He died in Paris in 1971 of an apparent heart attack at only twenty-seven, but no one, not even his family or bandmates ever saw his body and there was always a mystery surrounding his passing.

But we weren't looking for his body, we were hoping to find out about his skills.

He wasn't dead to us, we'd just seen him leading some friends to safety. The trick might be to find him sober.

*****

Over the next few days, I began researching footage of Doors' shows. It was hard not to choose shows to visit where the band was at the top of its game. The problem was that those shows most often involved an obviously very high Morrison. A case in point: I found footage of the band playing in New York in 1970. It's an amazing but poorly lit performance.

You see Morrison walk up to the mic and say, "how you doin' man?" He's talking to the audience as if they are all one person, and so they immediately become that. It's as if the twenty-thousand people are all friends in his living room. He then says, "Everything is fucked up as usual."

The audience cheers wildly and guitarist Robby Krieger begins the classic riff that starts 'Roadhouse Blues.' Morrison screams and spin jumps into the beginning of the song. When he comes in with the verse, it's everything we loved about him. His voice is raw and strong, and he is totally in the moment, almost sneering some of the lyrics.

People are now trying to get onstage to touch him, and there is a constant wave of roadies and security people pulling fans off the stage. Jim is soon lying on his back, singing to the sky, and rolling among those adoring fans like a kid at the beach. It reminded me of the Lizard King in the middle of all those dancing warriors. The audience was feeling that same crazy bliss. Mind you, this was the first song of the night.

So as much as I wanted to see that show in person, I couldn't hold out much hope of having a cogent conversation with a sober Morrison. I talked with Westlake about it and he agreed that we needed to find another moment.

Then I found an interview that keyboard player Ray Manzarek had done years after Morrison's death. In it he mentioned the 1970 Isle of Wight festival, and said that Jim, still reeling from an obscenity charge from a Florida show twelve days earlier, had decided to do the show sober. Bingo!

We had our destination, and as we hadn't yet shaved off our frontier beards, we would fit right into the early

Seventies look. At that point in time, many rockers and their fans affected the bearded unkempt look of young homeless people. Much like a few years later when spandex became the 'uniform' of pop music, and the torn jeans and leather jacket became the 'uniform' of punk rock, the long hair, beard, and often plaid shirts were the uniform of the early Seventies.

Westlake and I, looking period appropriate, stood near the old chair in front of the fountain. I had long since learned that the reason Westlake bought the mansion, was that a crossing of 'ley lines' passed through the property at the very spot where the chair now stood. Ley lines were supposed energy grids that could be found all over the planet by those in the know, and the chair seemed to be able to focus their power. I never thought to ask Westlake how he was able to find them, but he must have been taught by the very old professor who was his mentor years before.

"The Festival ran from Wednesday to Sunday, and about six hundred thousand people attended it. That's about a third more than Woodstock, which happened the year before," I said.

I was filling Westlake in on what I'd learned. Until I did the research, I hadn't realized the size and scope of the Isle of Wight festival. It was enormous.

"The lineup was pretty impressive. There were the 'they played Woodstock so we need 'em here too' folky types, John Sebastian, Richie Havens, and Melanie. There were a host of excellent or soon to be very famous Brit bands like Emerson Lake and Palmer, Supertramp, Procol Harum, Free, Ten Years After, and Family. And there were some of the biggest acts on the planet at that time, Chicago, The Who, Sly and the Family Stone, The Moody Blues, Jethro Tull, Jimi Hendrix, and of course The Doors."

As I read the list of bands to Westlake, I realized that I was almost drooling at the prospect of spending a few days seeing these wonderful bands, many of them in their prime but he brought me back to reality.

"I know you'd love it if we brought sleeping bags and stayed all five days but that's an indulgence I can't allow us. I've had to make deals with myself over the years. Deals that protect me from myself. One of those deals is that I form a question about some past mystery, and then try and solve it. If I was to go to Roswell and investigate that mystery, but then stay longer, because the weather was nice, I would feel that I was no longer a historian, but a tourist. I can't live that way. I hope you understand, Mike."

I did. I knew exactly what he meant. When you can go anywhere, you could theoretically go there for any reason. It would be the start of anything, anywhere goes, perhaps including insanity. (But I did take note of his mention of Roswell, and I filed it away for a later discussion.)

So it was decided that we would show up late Saturday afternoon, around the time that Ten Years After went on stage. That would give us time to work our way in, with Westlake's bogus back stage passes. We'd have a bit of time, because Emerson Lake and Palmer then went on...just before The Doors. It was a good plan, and it turned out better than we could have hoped for.

21

Light on Wight

"Humor keeps us alive. Humor and food. Don't forget about food. You can go a week without laughing."
   Joss Whedon

"Your fear is 100% dependent on you for its survival."
   Steve Mariboli

We jumped to a spot on the hill overlooking the stage, but quite a ways away. People up here weren't paying to get in but they still had a pretty good view. Some of them had taken the local farmer's hay bales and made shelters of them. Sounds pretty scratchy, and I'm guessing it was. They were calling it Desolation Row, after the Dylan song. Our landing spot was behind one of these hay huts, and unlike every other Westlake planned arrival we'd previously done, this one was witnessed. As we blinked into reality in front of the two young men, one said to the other, "far out man!...this is some really good shit."

From the hill we surveyed the immense gathering; it looked like a million people, or at least as many people as you've ever seen in one place. We could hear Ten Years After ripping up *'Goin Home'* as we walked down the hill. In the hour or so that it took us to get to the backstage area, we got to fully feel the vibe in the crowd.

It was electric. In years to come, the peace and love mantra of this generation would eventually become a thing of derision and scorn, but walking through this crowd it was alive. Ironically, many of these youngsters would grow up to be the very things they claimed, at

this point in their lives, to despise. But life is nothing, if not ironic.

We were offered more than a couple hits on more than a few joints as we made our way through the crowd. Westlake looked like everyone's favorite older hippy; ruggedly handsome, and with a thick head of hair but he politely waved away the weed offerings until we were just about at the gate to the back stage area. Then he was casually handed a pretty large spliff by some dude and rather than defer, he honked it, and then smiling, he handed it to me. This was obviously going to be a different time trip and one more at ease with my skills, although in retrospect, smoking weed, once again, wasn't one of them.

Westlake and I showed our credentials. We were supposed to be part of some free press bullshit thing that he made up, and we were let in to the backstage area. At that time in the world any press name mentioning the word 'free' was allowed almost anywhere, and Westlake had the charisma to get us in no matter who we supposedly represented.

The backstage area was a chaos of trailers, roadies, equipment trucks, and picnic tables with umbrellas, groupies, hangers on, and rock stars. We walked in and immediately bumped into Pete Townsend, who was apparently fretting about Roger Daltrey's tardiness.

"He said he'd be here by now! Where the fuck is he?" Townsend said to everyone and no one as he paced around in circles. They weren't going on for a few hours, but hey, we all find things to stress about.

There were groups of people chatting, drinking, and smoking weed. Some campfires had started since the sun went down, and people were gathering around them. I saw the great Paul Rodgers, lead singer of Free, talking with Donovan. I saw Joni Mitchell sitting at a table talking to some people, including Melanie and Patti Harrison. Sly Stone was holding court and Miles Davis, Leonard Cohen, Jimi Hendrix, and some guys from Chicago, were listening.

Then Keith Moon ran up to me and handed me a slice of watermelon. He had a crazy, gleeful look in his eye that said follow me. I was feeling pretty high from my spliff hit, so I did. He ran over to a table that had many slices of watermelon. He showed me how he wanted me to hold out the front of my shirt, and then he filled it with watermelon slices. Then he ran from group to group, me following, as he handed out melon slices from my shirt. It was pretty fucking stupidly awesome.

I looked back to see that Westlake was talking to Joni Mitchell, so I felt I could play on. I then heard the sound of a helicopter. Moon did too. He got a clever look in his eye and ran over to the table where we'd got the melons. He handed me an uncut half and grabbed one himself, and scurried over towards where the small copter was landing. He quickly positioned me to a spot, found his own spot and hefting the half melon, under the still turning helicopter blades, yelled, "one...two...three."

At that point, we both heaved our melons up into the blades just as Roger Daltrey, in white pants and shirt, and white cape, exited from the copter. He was immediately showered in a red fizz of watermelon. He was not happy. Moon ran off in glee but I fell to my knees laughing uncontrollably even knowing that I might be the subject of Daltrey's wrath. He gave me hardly a look before he ran screaming after Moon, his stained cape flying out behind him, making him look like a deranged super hero. I stayed there covered in watermelon fizz and laughing for a while before I could get up and walk. This was my kind of time travel!

I found some paper towels and cleaned off as well as I could and then headed back to where Westlake was standing and listening to one of the promoters, who looked like he'd been involved in a ship wreck.

"We're gonna lose our shirts on this. It's bad enough that the townsfolk changed our site location late in the game, and that everyone on the hill gets a free view, but those fucking French anarchists organized a group outside the gate to break the fences down," the promoter said through gritted teeth.

"They think the music should be free. They think the food should be free. Those cocksuckers probably think the planes and ferries that brought people over here should be free! Well there you have it. We are now a free fucking rock festival! Praise the Lord and pass the fucking bullshit!"

He continued his diatribe, but we'd heard enough. We walked away and came upon a short hairy young man pointing at and loudly trying to browbeat a defiant Joni Mitchel.

He was apparently the same guy who, earlier that afternoon, had grabbed the microphone away from her in the middle of her performance to begin a political rant. I was thinking that only a few years later, people like this would have been tackled long before they got to the mic. He was removed from the stage, but such were the times that many in the audience felt that he should have been allowed to speak. There were some boos from the audience, until Mitchell scolded them like the boorish children they were. History tells us that she completely won them over, and received an encore. It was a courageous performance but not only had the dolt not been thrown out, he was now back stage harassing the 'rich rock stars.'

"It's we the people who made you rich! And what do you give back?" the hairy man asked. "You charge us to see you play! Why can't you give to us freely from what you create?"

I was trying to follow his reasoning. Should a house painter paint houses for free? Should a cup cake maker do the same? We the people made lots of people rich. In most cases it's because they provided us a product or a service that we highly valued. Then I came to a realization about the guy. He was one self-righteous cunt.

Westlake then did a curious thing. He started walking backwards and waving his arms, all the while talking loudly to me. "Mike," he said, "it's as if this has become a temporary city of over half a million people! It is truly amazing!" I thought perhaps I was seeing him high and out of control for the first time. As it turned out, maybe not.

As he said the word 'amazing' he threw his arms straight out from his side, and his left elbow caught the shorter man on the side of the head. He went down like a cut flower.

Westlake looked shocked at this occurrence and immediately bent down to help the man back up, saying, "I'm so sorry! I didn't see you! In all this excitement I kind of forgot to watch where I was going. Please forgive me!"

The man wasn't hurt at all, other than perhaps his pride at falling off of his high horse. He grumbled something and wandered off, probably to berate some other performer.

Joni Mitchell looked at Westlake with a raised eyebrow. "I didn't ask for your help, and I didn't need it."

Westlake did a fair impression of an innocent man.

"I know you didn't need my help but then I didn't offer it. I'm just sometimes very clumsy."

Joni shook her head and smiled. "I doubt that."

We wandered further into the enclave, passing more campfires, musicians, and food wagons. John Sebastian and Donovan sat at a table playing a song I didn't recognize. Ten Years After had just finished their set, and Emerson Lake and Palmer were getting ready to go on. The Doors would be up after them. Still no Morrison...but he was back here somewhere.

We were hungry so we ate some hot dogs and drank some beer. I'd never seen Westlake so at ease as he was on this trip, but since all we had to do was talk to Morrison, there wasn't a lot we (or I) could fuck up. As for me, I was rubbing elbows with musicians I'd listened to all my life, so I couldn't have been happier. We took our beers, found a couple of chairs near a campfire and sat down. The night was becoming very cool and the warmth and crackle of the fire felt good. It wasn't quiet and restful; ELP were starting to pound it out on stage, but it was oddly relaxing, even a little ways away from the half million.

"Let's walk over there," Westlake said, rising from his chair.   We walked across an open space, side stepping some roadies muscling some large speakers and amps onto a ramp leading to the stage. I followed Westlake towards a shaded overhang and saw in the darkness the tiny bright light of a cigarette being inhaled. A voice came from the darkness.

"I see by the light and sparkle about you that you're not from around here," said the voice of Jim Morrison.

Westlake and I shared a look and walked into the dark spot and there he was. He was holding a bottle of Jack Daniels, which he passed to me. I took a pull on it and handed it to Westlake. So much for his keyboard player saying years later that Jim did the show sober. I turned and saw that he had a perfect view of the back stage thoroughfare from his current spot. He had probably been able to see our sparkling selves for a while. Westlake handed him back the bottle.

"We came here to talk to you, Jim," Westlake said.

Jim smiled, took a pull on the bottle and said, "of course you did." He seemed ready to hear what two time travelers had to say.

"We've noticed that you have some traveling skills that we are unacquainted with, and we hoped you would enlighten us," Westlake said.

It was so to the point that I was a bit stunned.

"Well.... this is the most refreshing conversation I've had all day," Morrison said. "I'm guessing that you two don't want an autograph." He said the last with a halfhearted smirk.

He seemed tired and distracted, but he was ready to continue. "What is it that you need to know from me?"

Westlake described our mode of travel, including ley lines and the old chair. He then mentioned us seeing Jim in 1804, (he left out the Bigfoot thing) and said that we knew he'd been there for weeks, which was something we couldn't do.

Jim's eyes came to life and he nodded and began to speak. "I don't recall seeing you two, but I tend to take a lot of mushrooms when I time trip. I don't know what you mean by lines, or an old chair. I was ten the first time it happened to me. The family was taking a car trip in the southwest when we stopped to camp in Colorado near the Four Corners. I was napping and ended up dreaming of an earlier time involving Conquistadors. I had no basis for the dream, because I knew nothing of Conquistadors, and maybe it was more than a dream, but it was real enough to spook me."

He stopped, took a draw from the bottle of Jack, swallowed hard and continued.

"It happened a few more times in my teens, and by then I started taking it serious. When I finally took LSD for the first time, it was there for me like an open book. I could envision a time and place and go there. I haven't gone too far back, just a few hundred years, and I refuse to try going into the future, but when this shit storm gets too heavy, I go somewhere to find relief."

I was speechless. All I could think was that Morrison was a human ley line. He could leave for anytime...at any time.

"Can I ask how you stay in one place for so long?" Westlake asked. "I can only stay for perhaps a week but it takes a lot out of me."

"That all happened by mistake," Jim explained. "Early on if I stayed too long I felt worn down like shit when I returned. But one time after staying too long when I was really ripped, I found that I couldn't concentrate enough to come back. I would get close and almost bump my return place, and then again...and again. After about four times, I finally returned and I felt surprisingly good. Over time, I practiced bumping back. It seems that if you come back all at once, you're body goes into shock, but if you come back gradually, over the course of five or ten minutes, your body becomes acclimated. At least it did for me. I'm pretty sure I could stay somewhere indefinitely. Someday I might try it and leave all this bullshit behind."

Just then Hendrix found us. He and Morrison hugged like the war buddies that they were. Jimi gave us a nod and took a slug from the bottle.

"Say hello to my friends, Jimi," Jim said.

"Hello, friends," Jimi said. "Listen, man, I've got some good shit if you want some."

Morrison declined and said, "No man, I'm gonna' do this one straight."

So that's what he meant by straight...alcohol but no drugs.

We'd learned what we needed to learn from Morrison, but it was hard to leave. I looked at Hendrix, who would be dead in three short weeks, and Morrison, who was by this time spiraling downward. I felt a great sadness that these wonderful talents would soon be gone but oddly, it almost seemed that their purpose had been somehow fulfilled. Hendrix had changed everything about rock guitar playing, but for the past few months had become almost a parody of himself, searching for his next big place.

Some said Morrison seemed changed by the bogus obscenity charge laid on him weeks earlier in Florida. But we had no basis for that comparison and found him to be honest and friendly to some fellow travelers.

We stayed for the show. Years later some reviewers would look back and call it subdued. Others would say that Morrison's demand that there be minimal lights on stage was because he was embarrassed by his appearance. All I can say is he looked fine to us and consider that he said this on a BBC radio interview the next day:

"I don't think our style holds up in a large outdoor setting. It's hard for us to make magic when we're not in a theater."

By bringing the lights down he was more likely trying to give the show a more intimate feel.

We watched totally enthralled as the band made a delicate but powerful magic. The last song they played was, of course, The End. It epitomized everything about the soon to be dead era of psychedelic music. The song was free flowing, with improvised tempo changes, and with Jim's lyrics and poetry gluing it together. At one point in that seventeen minute version, the band comes to an almost whispering stop, with just the slightest bit of keyboards and drums keeping it going.

A half a million people are holding their breath barely making a sound, held in the hand of The Lizard King as he sang-----This....is....the....ennnnnnd!

22

Machu Machu Man

"I hate to advocate drugs, alcohol, or insanity to anyone, but they've always worked for me."
Hunter S. Thompson

"If God dropped acid, would he see people?"
Steven Wright

It was sometime in the mid-80's and I was in the midst of some days off. We Fools were working so much that even a week off here and there seemed precious. I of course headed up to the mansion. It had been a while since I had tripped through time fantastic, so I was anxious to see what was up with Westlake and Hannah.

Remember that the way Westlake worked the time thing, we could leave and be away for three or four days, but return the same afternoon. I could theoretically only be away for an hour, but be spending days in another place.

Over some years I realized that while we had solved the physical reentry problem (with Morrison's help), the emotional drain was, at least for me, unsolvable. I could not go from my time spent, for instance, with Lewis and Clark in the wilderness and then get up on stage the next night in my own timeline. I tried once or twice and learned the hard way that it didn't work.

There was a very important aspect of it all that involved a sort of decompression. You had to put some time between yourself and the experience.

The fact that Westlake traveled so often, and yet stayed so even keeled, spoke volumes about his preparation and mental makeup. But then he was a historian and I was a guy in a band.

"Mike," Westlake said, opening the door to the mansion. "You're just in time. Come on in. Hannah, Mike's here!"

I know it sounds stupid for me to say it, considering his abilities, but I could never figure out how he always seemed to be expecting me, no matter when I arrived. In this case it had been a few months since our last encounter. Hannah appeared and there were hugs all around. We went out to the picnic table by the fountain and after some moments we reconnected. Maybe he was just a gracious host.

There was talk about how well my Dad was managing the property. There was talk about how well Gin and Hannah were getting along and they were both wanting to hear more stories about The Fools on the road and what new songs I was working on. All the while, like a kid waiting for dessert, I couldn't wait to turn the subject to the next time trip.

"So how about we check out Roswell? You must be curious about that?"

Me saying it out of the context of our comfortable conversation was pushy and uncool. I felt immediately that I had broken the moment, and I wanted to take it back. That's how I am sometimes, and the possibility of that trip was like a pastry almost within arm's length. (Hmmm...two mentions of food. I must be hungry.)

"Alright," Westlake replied, giving me a nod and smiling. "What about Roswell do you want to know and what mystery do you see us solving?"

It suddenly occurred to me that he might have already been there and seen it all. It made me once again consider Westlake's place in the universe and how well he handled it. Think of being able to go anywhere and see anything. All of life's mysteries could be solved but then think of having that power and the disconnect you would have with all of God's other creatures and especially us humans.

I think I stuttered but I said, "We could find out if it was a real alien crash, and solve that mystery." It sounded logical to me.

Westlake considered my answer for a moment and said this:

"I don't think it's any longer a mystery. Judging by what we went through with Merriweather Lewis there is no doubt that alien craft have been among us for at least centuries. Unless you discount what we saw with our own eyes back there, I would consider it case closed. They are here among us but don't worry, we would be dead long ago if they wanted us to be or so they told me."

"You talked to aliens?" I asked, astounded.

"No, Mike, I'm pulling your leg. I've never spoken to them...directly," he replied with a wink. "So what's our angle?"

I had no answer. He had plated it perfectly. I must have looked dejected because he stood up, whacked me on the shoulder, and said," There's other places we can go, and other things to learn."

With that we walked inside and headed towards his library.

From what I'd seen of the mansion, he ignored most of the many rooms in it. Other than the gym, the two rooms he most frequented were the billiards room and the library. He was a pretty good pool player, but he was a voracious reader. When he locked onto a subject he became single minded and read anything he could find about it.

The library itself was a classic old world example of what the well to do learned man would have in his home. It had floor to ceiling shelves whose contents were reached by an attached ladder. There must have been thousands of books on display. For anyone with a love of books, it was a virtual gold mine.

One sad aspect of such a beautiful room was that, with the eventual onset of the internet, it would soon become obsolete. Within twenty years of that day in the library, we would all have access at our fingertips to more information than a thousand such libraries could hold. We humans would once again sacrifice beauty for function and ease of operation...ah, but such is the way.

Westlake climbed the ladder to about fifteen feet up and after pulling it along sideways, he stopped and pulled a book from the shelf.

"This is the one," he said as he turned and tossed it to me. Without looking to see if I'd catch it (I did), he did a quick fireman's slide down with his feet on the outside of the ladder.

I looked at the book and saw that it was leather bound and old. It was called *Lost City of The Incas* by Hiram Bingham and opening the cover, I saw that it was published in 1948 and dealt with a Peruvian site that would eventually become one of the Seven Wonders of the Modern World.

"Read up on that. I think there's a mystery there to be solved. But don't just take Bingham's word on Machu Picchu, even though he discovered it, there are many interesting other opinions. Come back when you feel like you have a take on it."

So that's how I spent a good part of my week off, and a trip to the Ipswich library and a talk with Eleanor added enough other information to the point where I was fascinated by Machu Picchu. And the thought of traveling back there through time was once more intoxicating, but the reality of it was so much more.

23

The Stones and The Stoned

"I always wanted to be an explorer, but it seemed I was doomed to be nothing more than a very silly person."
Michael Palin

"So what have you learned?" Westlake asked, after we'd settled down at the table near the fountain with a couple beers. I looked out over the well-kept garden my Dad had placed about half way down the gentle slope of Westlake's back yard. It looked like it was thriving.

"Yes the tomatoes are doing well. Now what do you see us investigating?" Westlake asked.

I thought for a minute. Most of our trips began with me getting some form of a quiz, or an assignment to investigate. Ironically I hated high school and all forms of tests...but I loved this part of our process, maybe because there were no wrong answers. He knew that I too was fascinated by historical things unsolved, and it seemed his way of not only educating me, but getting me to focus on the subject in our headlights.

"Ok, I love that it's called The Lost City of The Incas, in that it survived The Spanish Conquest. Pretty much nothing else did."

Except for a few tiny enclaves, far from the epicenter, all of the Incan empire was devastated in a few short years by a relative handful of lunatic Christian gold hunting freaks from Spain. They were ruthless and relentless in their subjugation of the populace. Praise the Lord and pass the gold!

"I guess they never found it because it was located in the mountains at almost eight thousand feet and in the middle of nowhere," I added. "From what I've read, it's assumed by archeologists that it was built around 1450 AD, and that it was either a place of sacrifice or the summer retreat of an Incan king. Some stones involved weigh more than fifty tons so there's a curiosity about that. There's also been a few more female bones found than male bones so another school of thought has it as a place to sacrifice virgins. "

"Ah yes," Westlake said. "The active mind of the male academic. What else do you find curious about Machu Picchu?"

He, like me, was gazing down at the garden. Good job, Dad.

"Well, the odd thing is that there's no consensus as to why it was built, or for what reason." I was checking my notes. "And even the date is suspect. The Incas were adept at borrowing and absorbing the cultures of those they conquered, and some early chronicles even suggest that they were opportunistic, much like the Egyptians, about claiming the past for their own. So the place could be much older. There's even a local legend that the place was built in one night by giants."

"The tomatoes are really happening," Westlake said, gazing down the yard, "your father has the greenest of thumbs. But is there anything else that you find curious about the site?"

I was saving this for last, as much because it was my final take on the subject as that I was enjoying making him wait to see if I had picked the most astounding aspect of the place.

"What I don't get is how the builders, supposedly with bronze tools, and without the wheel, (for Christ sake), not only carried some of these huge stones up a few thousand feet from a quarry, but also fashioned those stones together so that you cannot fit a knife blade between them. There are some stones with lots of angles, but there's not a lot of explanation as to why. Some say the angles were for more stability during earthquakes, but that wouldn't explain a rock with over thirty cut angles. It's almost as if the builders were showing off."

I paused for a moment and thought. "And finally, it was really hard rock that they were dealing with, and some of those very hard stones are polished smooth. I know that sand can be used to polish rock, but then the man hours involved make the job seem ridiculous. The standard explanations just don't make sense."

Westlake had been staring at the garden while I talked, but as soon as I stopped, he said "you got it. That's what we're going to go back and find out. I'm hoping we can even bring Jim along. I've been trying to find him."

24

The Hills Are Alive With the Sound of Very Loud Music

"I don't believe in astrology, I'm a Sagittarius and we're skeptical.
Arthur C. Clarke

"We never really grow up, we only learn how to act in public."
Bryan White

It was the first I'd heard that Jim Morrison was still alive...somewhere. Although I'd heard the rumors, it made my head spin.

"So he didn't die in Paris?" I asked.

"He may have, Mike, but I've seen him here and there down the time line since."

"How is that possible?"

"As you know, he has skills that we've only learned a small part of and he did tell us that if things got crazy, he might travel and never come back. So maybe he is lying dead in a cemetery in France, or maybe he is traveling in time. Or maybe both things are true."

It was stunning news to me, but I got the point. There was so much we didn't know about Morrison.

"I'm confused. When in time are we going to that place and why is Jim a part of it?"

"I hope we're going to when it was built," Westlake explained. "I went back a very long time, well before the supposed time it was made, and still it existed. I got a few thousand years back before I found nothing there. Then I found a time when the place had been cleared and ready for building. I'm hoping to have you put us there in the time it was built. "

"But why Jim?" I asked.

Understand that he is on my Mount Rushmore of singers...well maybe if there were five or six heads instead of four, but in my mind that's still a tiny elite community. I was excited at the possibility of seeing him again, but Westlake and I talked about every aspect of everything we did on a travel and this was no different.

"I have a feeling about Jim," he said. "I know he is erratic and at times unbalanced, but he is also brilliant and fearless. I recently found him hanging out at Lincoln's Gettysburg address. By the way, Lincoln was amazing in person, both in charisma and as an orator, even though, oddly enough, he had a relatively high pitched voice.

Jim was there as a calm student of the day. That's the guy I hope we can bring along and maybe we can learn a thing or two about his methods so I'm headed back to Gettysburg to try and enlist his aid. I'll call you as soon as I know what's up."

"Sounds good. Wait a minute...earlier you said that I was going to put us in the right time."

"That's right. It's time for you drive, Mike."

I went home and my nerves were on edge. What if I frigging put us in the middle of a volcano or the middle of some ancient battle? Westlake had been teaching me for a while to drive and use the Akashic ribbon that weaves through time, but was I ready? If you asked me, I needed more time.

It was the next evening that I got a call from Westlake. He said simply, "Can you be ready to leave in the morning?"

I remember dreaming that night of dark swirling shapes. It wasn't a restful sleep, but then, I never sleep well the night before a travel and the idea that I was going to be the one to move us through time didn't help.

I arrived at the mansion at around seven to find Hannah and Westlake having their morning coffee out back near the fountain. It was just another day in the life of these two time travelers. I noticed that the chair was in place. It gave me the usual slight shudder of excitement mixed with apprehension.

"Hey, Mike," Westlake said with no buildup. "He says he'll meet us there. He also said he would meet you at the place you mentioned. Do you know what he might be talking about?"

I was clueless but then Jim did tend to say some crazy shit that neither of us could quite figure out.

Westlake was in travel mode, focused on our destination, so he got me quickly in gear. He gave me a handful of slightly dried green leaves.

"Chew these," he said. "They'll help you with the elevation. We'll be at eight thousand feet. It's not like snorting it backstage before a gig, but it'll have the same affect. "

That was Westlake giving me shit about my former drug use as he handed me the coca leaves. For you who don't know, cocaine is the processed end result of coca leaves. Some of us did a bit of that back in the day. It's nothing to be proud of, but if you're going into high up elevations it can be beneficial. The Incas used it. Their own form of the pony express had runners, using coca leaves, to increase their ability to run and deliver messages over long distances. Anyhow, let's just say that I had a nostalgic moment or two when I chewed the leaves.

We messed around a bit but as usual, Hannah helped us prepare. Even with Westlake's info, there was no way to dress like we belonged. Who knew what that look was so we went with dungarees, t-shirts, and ball caps; the outfit of the well-traveled man. Westlake had picked a landing spot for us that he hoped would allow us a non-intrusive over view. Finally as crazy as it seemed to me, Morrison was to meet us there.

I sat in the chair and Westlake cleared his throat. I slowly stood and shrugged.

"Are you sure this is a good idea?" I asked. "I mean, going back to the sixties is one thing, but going back thousands of years..."

Westlake interrupted. "It's no different than going back to the sixties. Time travel is time travel, Mike. If I didn't think you were ready, then we wouldn't be having this conversation."

We switched places and I began to concentrate just as I had been taught. I closed my eyes and Boom!

I opened them to see we hadn't gone anywhere. I let out a disappointed sigh.

"Try again. Clear your mind and picture where we want to be," Westlake said. "I have faith in you."

I looked over at Hannah and she smiled and nodded. For whatever reason, that calmed me and I tried again.

I nailed it and we landed exactly where Westlake had planned.

As I caught my breath, I became aware of a loud droning sound, almost but not quite like the low throated chant of Gregorian monks.

We were on a hill looking down at an amazing sight. There were a dozen or so enormous men and women, somewhere between seven and nine feet tall. They were all wearing gray robes, except for one woman who was wearing a turquoise robe, and they all had the sparkle of time travelers. They were making that droning noise as they walked across an empty plain, the turquoise woman in the lead. Though I knew by the adjacent scenery that we were in the right place, there were no stone buildings or stone walls.

"Giants" I whispered to Westlake, although with the droning going on there was no chance of my being overhead.

We were not more than fifty yards away from them as they walked passed. They were all olive skinned, very attractive, and majestic in their appearance. They were proportioned like athletes and walked with an innate nobility. A few of them were carrying what looked to be large two pronged tuning forks. Some others were carrying long thin horns.

The woman in the lead carried a clear crystal globe that seemed to shimmer as it picked up the color of her robe. She took them to a gradual incline that led to a fifteen foot high up cropping of rock that was literally part of the mountain. She climbed up easily onto it and placed the globe in the air, a foot above the up cropping, and made a casual wave at it with her hand. Amazingly, it stayed there in the air when she took her hands away and climbed down. The droning continued. Westlake and I looked at each other open mouthed.

She stood there while the others, still droning their chant, formed a circle around her. Shortly the droning abruptly stopped. There was a moment of quiet, and then those carrying horns began blowing them. The deal seemed to be that the six of them would blow loudly, but one after another, and that when one was almost out of breathe, another would start, so that the note never ended. I don't know what note they were playing, but Rich tells me the universe vibrates in the key of A (440 kHz) so maybe that's what they were blowing.

Anyhow, the horns were deafening. I thought about the Biblical account of the horns blowing down the walls of Jericho. They might have been this loud. I noticed that, like me, Westlake had his fingers in his ears.

They aimed their sound at the globe hanging in the air. The others holding the tuning forks pointed them toward the globe. All the while the turquoise woman stood there not far from the now pulsating globe, waiting. The horns blew shorter notes until one player was musically on the heels of another. The tuning fork people were now having to hold their trembling forks with both hands. The horns players joined together in an enormous extended blast and the air around the

globe exploded into a vision. It was Macho Picchu as we see it now. The vision hung there in the sky and the

turquoise lady studied it for a moment.

Then she began waving her hands and rocks around her exploded into shape. Enormous stones flew through the air and were instantly cut and placed by her vision. She was dancing as she brought the stones about, some of them from atop the mountain, and some of them from very far away. We watched gigantic stones crest the side of the hill and hang in space for a moment until she chose their place. It was a rock ballet like no other. In a very short time, her vision changed all we saw into another shape. We watched as the world changed and we were transfixed.

In the midst of this it occurred to me that Morrison wasn't with us, but I said nothing to Westlake. Maybe Jim forgot about the request or was too high to do it. Both were strong possibilities.

But then we saw him, walking across the plain towards the turquoise lady, dancing his way carefully through the circle of horns and tuning fork people. She was oblivious at first but then, with half of the world spinning in her hands, she turned to see him.

"Jesus fucking Christ," Westlake said. "What is he doing?"

Morrison walked casually up to the enormous woman and, while she held the shaping world in her hands, he started waving his, as if explaining something. Her creation of things paused for a moment, but then as if almost to impress our friend, the world exploded in a hundred directions. Walls formed, buildings took shape, and stairways happened between them all.

To us, it looked a speeded up stop action film but the last thing she did, before she looked away from him, was point to a large rock and make it complicated. With whatever mental skills she had, she kept cutting extra angles into it, until there were well over thirty. At that point she placed it in a wall and made all the stones around it fit.

Satisfied with her brilliance, she looked at those she'd come with, surveyed all she'd done, and with them all, she blinked out of existence. The globe remained, and then as if guided by an unseen hand, glowed very brightly and carved the stone beneath it into an odd shape. Then it too blinked out of existence. I learned later that the carved shape has been for ever after called *Intihautana*, or 'the hitching post of the sun.' If you ever get to Machu Picchu, you'll see it.

But what of Jim you ask? Well I'm not really sure. When the turquoise lady was creating the world, it was hard to see anything else. She may have had him spinning at some point, but maybe that's just a dream I had years later. I know this though, when the dust cleared that day, thousands of years ago, and Westlake and I fixed upon a newly built Machu Picchu, Jim was nowhere to be found. Westlake seemed a little put off by it. Maybe because it was a personal invite, and though Jim came, he never connected with us. Me I see it this way; I've since gotten to visit Machu Picchu in my real life and I had the great pleasure to walk up to a stone, and though I know we travelers can't change time, I looked at a stone that has more than thirty impossible angles in it, and wondered if it wasn't caused because my friend Jim disturbed a certain lady.

Yeah, that's how I see it.

25

The Basket Weave

"A man is not old until regrets take the place of dreams."
John Barrymore

"Remorse is the poison of life."
Charlotte Bronte

Some years went by. There were many other time travel adventures that I may get to at some later point. Let's just say that I learned that all is not always what it appears to be. I thank Westlake for showing me, not only some great moments of the past, but my own opportunities, minus my fears.

The Fools traveled a large part of the world, excluding South America, Australia, Central Asia, China, both North and South Poles, all of the islands in the South Pacific, and all parts of Africa. Okay, maybe we missed a lot of it, but at the time it felt like a large part of the world.

I was trying to find a way to weave all these stories together, or even get everything under one umbrella, or at least in one basket. So many stories, and so many people light up the memory noggin. But it came to this.

It was the late 90's and we Fools had broken up, well not that really, we had just decided to stop playing. It was painful, but at the time it seemed right (it would last all of eight months). By then, Gin and I had been for some years in southern New Hampshire. While we were in intermittent contact with Westlake and Hannah, we were busy raising our daughter Sara.

So I was stunned one day when Hannah showed up at our door near to tears. Odd as it seems, while Gin had met her many times over the years at one restaurant or another, I'd never seen her outside of the mansion...and I'd never seen her so stressed.

"I need your help Mike," she said.

I should mention now that while I was then into my late forties, and she should have been at least ten years older, she looked ten years younger. It was the same with Westlake, I'd watched myself over time pass him in age. It was perhaps that they spent so much time away from our time that it slowed their aging process.

So as not to cause confusion among the locals, they both took pains to look older. They dyed gray streaks in their hair, and each had taken to wearing glasses that neither one of them needed. We all dealt with it as best we could, but it was strange. The good thing about it was that it forced me to constantly acknowledge something that, even after all these years, I would try and find some way to disbelieve. Pretty stupid huh?

"He should have been back by now. He always comes back on the day he left. It's been three days now and I don't know what to do. I would go and look myself but...I'm pregnant."

I was stunned for a moment. Though I'd known for years that they were a couple, and loved each other very much, I guess I thought of them as being outside the normal processes of everyday humanity. It was also a little weird for someone trying to pass as a grandmother looking person to tell you she was pregnant.

She continued. "I can't risk taking a baby back through time. Especially not to that place." She was crying now.

It was hard to see. She was a strong woman and she was my friend. We brought her in and sat her down. Gin gave her a glass of water and told her how happy she was to hear the news of her pregnancy. She drank some water and slowly calmed down.

"What place?" I asked. "Where did he go?"

She took a deep breath and slowly exhaled. "The Battle of the Bulge," she replied. "He went back to find out something to help your Dad."

"What!?" I almost yelled. "How was he helping my Dad?"

Westlake had told me many times over the years that he avoided going into hostile environments, and while we'd encountered danger on some of our trips, it was generally inadvertent. Going to one of the more deadly battles of World War II though was begging for trouble.

"Your father and Patrick have become good friends over the years, to the point where your father has confided in him about his war experiences." Hannah explained.

My Dad was now almost eighty, and though he'd retired from his job as caretaker at the mansion, he still kept a small garden and a dozen or so chickens on the property that he and my Mom would tend.

"As far as I know, he hates talking about the war," I said.

It bugged me a little that he was telling his war tales to someone other than my brother John and I. To us, he would occasionally tell a story, but not too much of substance. He avoided talking about battles and talked more about how much he liked many of the civilians he met in both France and Germany.

"Why didn't he ask me to go along?" I asked.

I knew that both Alex and John, the men I'd seen years before carrying the time chair, had both long since retired. Of the two of them, John had been the one to occasionally join Westlake on a trip, but most often it was Hannah. I knew I wasn't his first choice, but with Hannah unable to travel, I thought I was at least on his list.

"Don't take it personally," Hannah said. "There were a number of reasons why he couldn't take you along. You know that he wouldn't put you in harm's way, but he was also uncomfortable putting you in the same timeline as your father years before you were born. But first and foremost, he would be breaking a trust. Your father told him a very personal and painful story that he'd apparently kept to himself all these years. When Patrick heard it, he felt it was something he needed to investigate. Of course your father doesn't know about our...abilities, he was just sharing a story with a friend."

I thought about it for a minute. "It was war. I'm sure he saw things and had to do things that are probably almost impossible to forget, if not reconcile. What kind of story would cause Patrick to travel back there and investigate?"

"Your father is a very funny, engaging man, but there's always been a sadness about him," Hannah explained.

It wasn't a revelation to me. Periodically over the years, I'd seen him gaze off at nothing. It was that 'thousand yard stare' that was not uncommon in war veterans who'd seen a lot of action.

She continued. "Patrick at some point over the years had asked your Dad why he hadn't kept in contact with his Army buddies. I know that your mother and you and your siblings had encouraged him to attend the reunions that were held every few years, but he always refused to go. It seemed odd that such a social man would not want to reconnect with others who'd shared a common experience."

"To be honest, it's always felt odd to me too," I said.

"Yes, so a few weeks ago, after a couple of beers, your Dad told Patrick a story. It's apparently the reason why he'll never attend a reunion, or make an effort to contact any of the men from his company."

"What reason? What happened?" I was on the edge of my seat.

"Your Dad is convinced that he killed his best friend at the Battle of the Bulge," Hannah said sadly.

"Jeezus," I said, barely above a whisper.

26

Old Soldiers Come Home

"The only thing we have to fear is fear itself."
Spoken thoughts of FDR prior to WW11

"Actually there's quite a few things we should be terrified about; for one, were going to enter a World War, and for another, Germany, Italy, and Japan are teamed up against us. It sucks and we should be very afraid."
Private thoughts of FDR prior to WWII

"Heroism often results from extreme events."
James Geary

My Dad was a war hero. He left Ipswich as a young man from a small town, and thirty-three months later he returned, much older than the time spent over there should have made him. But maybe that's because it wasn't a long vacation. Like many in his generation, he signed up to fight the day after Pearl Harbor. We were a country at war and our best young people were leaving tiny towns, huge cities, and every place in between. In some ways, it was the most unifying event ever to happen to our country.

My Dad's war journey started in North Africa, and then went on to the D-Day landing on a beach in

Normandy, and then finally through France and into Germany.

Over the course of that almost three year journey, he contacted malaria, single handedly captured a German

soldier, made strong friendships with other soldiers and saw more than a few of them die.

Those of us who've never been in armed conflict have no conception of what it must be like to bond with the same group of comrades, some of them since boot camp, and then watch them die. We have all lost friends suddenly. Life takes them from us in numerous ways; car accidents, medical traumas, and unexpected demises. Few of us however, outside of the military, have had the 'he's dead but we gotta move on' experience. My Dad did, more than once.

Over time he rose to the rank of Master Sergeant. At one point he was wounded, but after seeing many with more serious injuries, he refused a Purple Heart.

There is a picture of him from that time period that my family treasures. I carry a copy of it in my wallet. He's standing over a foxhole, almost smiling, with his hat at an 'I'm cool' angle and him looking full of life. I like to think of it as him being proud of his looks, and also his uniform.

Later down the line, he got drunk and stole a general's jeep and got busted back to private. We'll get back to that later.

"So did Patrick tell you about his landing spot," I asked Hannah, "the Battle of the Bulge went on for a month."

I was stressed and wanting to pick my landing place correctly, knowing I couldn't spend weeks, or even days looking for him without putting myself into further jeopardy than this trip would already incur. Hannah was telling me what she knew, but I was still looking for the window. The Akashic ribbon of eternity, which holds the information and data of all time, is accessible, but only if you have the keys.

After years of traveling with Westlake, he gave me those keys. Let's just say, I could now drive the chair by myself, and for Westlake's sake, I was hoping he had taught me well.

"He said it was towards the end," Hannah explained. "They were retreating through the Ardennes forest and your father's unit was low on ammunition and near to being overrun by the Germans."

It's ironic because the Ardennes was the place considered so safe that it had a training facility for new arrivals and a rest area for units that had seen too much hard fighting. My Dad's group was among the latter. It must have freaked them all out when a major, can we save our German asses, offensive came busting through their area. They had no choice but to retreat, and they did, by the thousands, fighting their way through the thick forests, many of them facing combat for the first time.

For the Germans, already pushed to the brink on the east by the Russians, it was a possible game saver. They were hoping to split the Allied forces, and retake Antwerp. The weather was foggy and bad enough that the build-up of German forces wasn't observed from the sky.

In the days prior to the attack, German paratroopers, wearing the uniforms and dog tags of captured G.I.s, and fluent in English, dropped into the forest. It was their mission to change sign posts, misdirect traffic, and cause confusion. When the attack came, it was a total surprise, and because it pushed a wedge seventy miles wide and fifty miles deep into Allied lines, it soon became known as the Battle of the Bulge.

This would be the bloodiest conflict suffered by American forces during the war. There would end up being an estimated eighty-two thousand American casualties. Of those, nineteen thousand were killed, nearly fifty thousand wounded, and twenty-three thousand were missing or captured. It's all just numbers, but the heartbreak and stories that have spun off of those numbers have lasted for generations.

Many heroes didn't make it home. My Dad would wonder until the end of his days why he'd been chosen to survive, maybe only because the bullets flying at them were so indiscriminate. Lucky I guess, because I wouldn't be here if he wasn't, but my Dad had a thing about him. In his own way he was a very street smart kid, and at least to some small degree it probably helped him survive.

"They had retreated to Bastogne but it wasn't going well," Hannah added. "It was very foggy and there was a foot of snow on the ground. On the edge of town they were ordered to dig in. The German forces soon had the town and area around it surrounded. There would be no more retreating. Patrick thought the incident must have taken place somewhere in the days between December 20 and 27. That's when Bastogne was surrounded. He went as a war correspondent working for the Associated Press. He had credentials but you know him, he could talk his way into anything. Oh, Mike what if he's hurt or worse!"

She was again full on crying. Ginny was comforting her, but to be honest, I had the same thought...Westlake was, for whatever reason, unable to return, and none of the reasons for that would be good. I'd thought more than once about our risks during time travel. Dying somewhere in the past was certainly one of them.

I'd learned long ago that when people are freaking out, it's good to give them a task. I too was freaking out. I've always called him Westlake, but it shouldn't make it seem like we weren't the best of friends. We were, so I too needed a task.

"Hannah, I have a plan, but I'll need you to dress me appropriately. You'll need to make me look like an AP reporter from WWII. I'm going to need whatever bogus credentials Patrick had, and I'm going to need a weapon appropriate to the time. And live ammo please."

Gin gave me a look and I knew exactly what she was thinking. We had a young daughter now and I wasn't exactly a man of action...I was a frigging musician, but we both knew this had to be done and there was no one else who could do it.

And so Gin drove Hannah's car and I followed in ours as we went from our house in New Hampshire to the mansion in Ipswich. We had replaced despair with a plan and that made us all more upbeat.

Hannah dressed me in the appropriate attire, including black horned rimmed glasses to make me look studious. I was also equipped with a note book, and a loaded Walther P38 hand gun which was inside my belt and covered by my coat, and a helmet. I felt ready to go, but something felt missing in our plan.

"I need someone else to go with me," I blurted out, "I need to go find Jim."

And I did, in a place I was apparently destined to go. But at that point in my life, only Jim Morrison knew that.

27

Honest Abe and Jim

"I'm a success today because I had a friend who believed in me, and I didn't have the heart to let him down."
Abraham Lincoln

"If a man comes to the door untouched by the madness of the Muses...he and his sane compositions...are utterly eclipsed by the performances of the inspired madman."
Socrates.

I knew where Jim was, at least for a while in time, and I knew that he was (relatively) sober when Westlake met him at Lincoln's Gettysburg address. Years earlier, Westlake found him at that place and asked him to join us at Machu Picchu. In a way he did but there was a comment from that time that I never figured out. Jim told Westlake that he would 'meet me' at a place we talked about. For years, I had no clue as to what place he meant, but over time I came to think of it as just some trippy Jim thing.

Now I knew what place it was, it was Gettysburg, where I would ask him for help. My goal was to show up well before Lincoln spoke, but find Jim somewhere in the place. Going early, I hoped, would keep me from meeting Westlake, which would only confuse everything. I couldn't meet Patrick years before I was trying to save him. It's complicated.

Hannah dressed me appropriately; in spite of the late fall heat in Pennsylvania, most everyone was wearing a dark suit and a hat. My hat was a perfect example of the era, and I couldn't help but check myself in the mirror. The suit and hat were just right, especially the hat. I also had about fifteen bucks in 1860's currency, not much by today's standard, but back then it had the buying power of over four hundred dollars. In other words, it was a tidy sum. I stood behind the chair, as if someone was in it, and worked my way down the time line. I concentrated, and boom! I was someplace else.

*****

I should have picked a landing spot away from the gathering, but my traveling skills were not all that developed. Then again it's not the worst thing to land in the middle of a crowd. Each one thinks you pushed your way in front.

And that's how I found my way to November 19, 1863...at about eleven o'clock in the morning. I know that because as I was standing there in the midst of a very smelly human throng, I saw the great man riding towards me on a great chestnut mare.

There was something about him, as he rode that horse wearing his customary stovepipe hat that was ungainly and almost goofy. In a way it was a Stan Laurel kind of thing (look him up). One reporter from that time period would mention his 'involuntary comical awkwardness.'

At the same time he had a natural grace that was

certainly at odds with his gait, and it gave him a complexity that must have added to his appeal.

I pushed my way through the crowd so that I would be close as he rode by. He wasn't far away when all the men were 'uncovering ' which was the term back then for taking off your hat in deference to someone or something. I did the same. The hat not only felt good on my head, it felt good in my hand.

He nodded and smiled at the well-wishers, of which there were many, and tried to ignore the occasional heckle, of which there were a few. The nature of the event, to celebrate dead soldiers, seemed to keep both the cheering and jeering to a modest degree.

It struck me standing there, that long ago, we used to be a country where anyone could approach and even talk to the elected leader of us all. I was later to learn that Lincoln had a single security guard, and sometimes rode his horse alone among the populace. What a charming vision from our past. A few assassins changed it all.

Like most, I've seen his few pictures but they do no credit to the man. He had a charisma about him that pictures can't portray. He rode comfortably through the crowd but as he came closer, I noticed that he looked flushed and tired. I didn't know it that day, but I would later learn that he had recently contracted a mild form of smallpox that would soon see him bedridden for almost a month. Yet to be diagnosed by his doctor, all he knew on this day was that he felt lousy. Though he was ill, he was still Abraham fucking Lincoln goddammit, and in about three hours he would deliver one of the most poignant and moving speeches on liberty, sacrifice, and statehood in the history of recorded man.

As he finally rode near me, looking pleasantly on all who had come, his eyes met mine. Then an odd thing happened. He seemed to pull back for a second, and he held my gaze longer than you'd expect but with a questioning look. He slowed his horse almost to a stop and I looked up into his eyes, which seemed all knowing and deep as a canyon. My first thought was that I must not look like I belonged. I dismissed it instantly because Hannah was so good at putting you properly dressed in any time period.   Then I wondered if he saw my sparkle...the kind of thing only travelers see. Was Lincoln a traveler, or was he sensing something different about me? It was more likely the latter. He was, after all, said to have a bit of the second sight about him. In our time we call that ESP.

In any event, I nodded up at him, he seemed to make a decision about me, and he rode on. As amazing as it was to stand that close to a legend, I was here to meet another legend, Jim Morrison and I needed to avoid meeting a very good friend of mine. What could I say to Westlake if I saw him? In his real time, he was here to invite Jim to Machu Picchu, something now years in the past, and my father was yet to confide in him in the future about his war experience. Its head spinning I know. Mine certainly was.

I walked a little away from the speaking platform up to a small hill and looked down on the assembled thousands. To my great surprise I saw, sprinkled among the crowd, more than a handful of sparkling people! I had learned earlier that it wasn't only Westlake and

Morrison who'd solved the mystery of time travel. This was obviously a popular traveler destination. As I looked out at the crowd, I was too far away to identify which sparkle was Morrison, or worse yet, Westlake.

I'd thought all I'd have to pick out was a couple of sparkling people. This complicated the matter. I looked around me and saw a man with a spy glass over to my right. He was a portly fellow, and well whiskered, and he seemed to be enjoying what he was seeing. I walked over to him. I needed his spyglass.

"Are you looking at him?" I asked the man.

"Am I looking at who, sir," he replied giving me a sideways glance, and getting back to his viewing.

"Are you looking at Mr. Lincoln?" I asked as if talking to a child.

"I have no interest in that man," the fellow said.

He was obviously irritated by my interruption in his viewing but then I thought I'd found an angle. There were some attractive women in the crowd, so maybe if he wasn't looking at Lincoln, he might be having his 1863 voyeur moment...and I needed his spyglass.

"There are some pretty women out there," I said, giving him what I thought was a conspiratorial leer and trying to connect with him. He stopped his viewing and turned to look at me with a scowl.

"Have you escaped from somewhere sir? Are there people in pursuit of you? If so I would suggest that you run off before they catch you."

This was not going well, but I needed his spyglass, so I took the leap.

"I'll give you ten dollars for your spyglass," I said.

He gave me a careful look. "We both know that my spyglass is not worth a quarter of that sir. It you want so desperately to look at women, why not get nearer to the scene and climb a tree? They would all be there below you, and you can have your way with the limb you are clinging to while you watch them."

It was getting late in the morning and I needed his spyglass so I said, "I'll give you fifteen dollars."

He studied me carefully and then said this:

"It's not my policy to take advantage of people of a simple nature, and especially those with obvious perversions, and being as how you appear to be both of those, but also a man of means, I will accept your offer, on the condition that you include that fine hat."

I didn't care about the money, but I'd grown fond of the hat. However it was getting late and I had no choice. I paid the scoundrel the money and gave him my hat, before he could also demand my jacket and pants.

Before he left I asked him, "Who were you looking at?"

"Why Edward Everett of course! He's simply the greatest orator of our time." He said this while adjusting his new hat to his head. "Now if you'll excuse me, he seems headed for the podium, so I will make my way in that direction. Upon arriving, I will doff this fine hat in his direction."

I watched him and my hat make their way jauntily down the hill. I raised my hard bought spyglass and looked out on the crowd. I concentrated on the people with sparkles about them. I saw an older man making his way towards Lincoln. I saw a man and woman who might have been the Sony and Cher dressed looking couple I'd seen years before at the Van Morrison concert in Boston. I saw an Asian man of middle years standing near the podium as Everett began to speak....but still there was no sight of Jim.

Everett would speak for almost two hours prior to Lincoln's remarks. His speech was well received. Lincoln, in contrast, spoke for only a couple of minutes. There are only ten sentences in the Gettysburg address containing two hundred and seventy-two words. Everett would later say that Lincoln "better stated the reason for the dedication...in two minutes than I was able to do in two hours."

It was almost two hours into Everett's speech and I was still periodically scanning the crowd for any new sparkly arrivals, when I felt a tap on my shoulder. I turned to see Jim Morrison standing there, dressed in an ill-fitting gray suit and wearing a cap. His hair was of moderate length and he had a short beard. He was smiling at me. I instantly realized that his outfit was more appropriate than mine. I looked like a well to do dandy, although one who must have lost his hat. He looked like a poor man here to see the President.

"I could see you sparkling from halfway across the field; it's Mike right?" He shook my hand and gave me a friendly half hug. "I come here often to hear him speak. It never gets old. And I like just walking among humans. I can't do that in my time."

He said it without the slightest anger or resentment towards the fan mob who'd made it impossible for him to walk anywhere unbothered, except maybe Paris.

I got right to it. "Westlake is lost in time and I need your help. I can't do it alone."

Jim looked at me thoughtfully and then said, "Over here."

We walked to a large tree a ways back from the gathering. Jim sat himself down and motioned for me to do the same. He then lit a joint, and passing it to me. "Tell me it all."

I took a hit, and I did.

It was some good shit and I found myself shortly babbling about way too many things. I meant to just tell him how a fellow traveler was lost in time, but he was a good listener, and he asked the right questions. Soon I was telling him things like Westlake giving me a graduation present so that I saw the Beatles as a teen. Jim liked that.

"In that case, had you looked around that night you might have seen me," he said, handing the joint back to me.

Then we started laughing, at first probably at the quirks of our crazy time travel existence, and then at everything in general. We laughed like happy idiots and when the people walking by took notice, we laughed all the harder til we cried. It was about the best stoned half hour I've ever had.

Then I mentioned Lewis and Clark and seeing him dancing with the warriors and he got quiet. Yeah I can be a buzzkill.

"They were my people. When I knew that saucer was coming, I had to get them out of there." He spoke as if reliving it, just like I was. "I didn't know the old man was left behind until I came back and found out Lewis and you guys saved him. I know about bouncing realities and changing time lines, but we take responsibility for whatever one we are in. What you guys did was far out. And I will do whatever I can to help you retrieve Westlake."

That's what I'd come to hear so I showed Jim the Army picture of my Dad and told him about what happened at The Battle of the Bulge, and how Westlake had gone back to learn the details and days later he hadn't returned. I was getting emotional talking about it. Jim thought for a moment and then said this:

"Ok man, we gotta be cool about this. I've got a plan. But before I tell you, we have to be ready for the strong possibility that your friend is dead. There's some bad shit flying around that place. They're getting shelled, shot at, they're under constant attack, and they're running low on ammo. It's why I stay clear of violent places. But if he's there, and alive, we'll find him and bring him back."

I'd never seen this side of Jim. He was focused, rational, and level headed...a man of action. I realized immediately that he would be leading this expedition, and I felt a great relief that such an experienced time traveler was going to be in charge.

He was standing now and pacing back and forth as the plan was apparently taking shape in his mind, and the excitement of the adventure took hold of him.

"We're going to need some outfits. And I'll of course need to visit the place we are returning him to, so I can form the picture in my mind of its location. There should be a doctor waiting there for us upon our return, in case any of the three of us are injured or incapacitated."

I told him about the mansion and about Hannah, and her almost limitless supply of costumes and outfits.

"Excellent! You know I was once tempted as a young man to join the service. It'll be good to wear the uniform."

For the first time since Hannah had come to my house in tears, I was feeling like we could actually pull this crazy mission off. I knew that coming here and asking for his help was a gamble, who knew what mental state he would be in? But the man I saw now gave me hope. Then he said this:

"You know my Dad was an admiral and he used to let me fire a machine gun off of his aircraft carrier."

I looked at him and my shoulders slumped. "Jeezus, Jim, if you're gonna make shit up, at least make it believable! Did you just drop acid? Damn!"

Jim laughed and said, "Let's go meet Hannah."

And we did.

28

The Boys Are Back in Town

"They've got us surrounded again...the poor bastards."
Col. Creighton S. Abrams
Tank commander at the Battle of the Bulge

"Bran thought about it. 'Can a man still be brave if he's afraid?'
'That is the only time a man can be brave,' his father told him."
George R. R. Martin, *A Game Thrones*

I know it seems like I'd been wasting time since Hannah told me about Westlake, but I was back about an hour after I left for Gettysburg. That's how you can work time travel; you can be gone for days and return an hour after you left. It's your choice. When I returned I wasn't alone.

Jim arrived with me with eyes wide open. He knew he was a ways into the future and I could see that it was freaking him out. Like Westlake, he apparently preferred to avoid future travel, so this was new stuff but he was gracious to both Hannah and Gin.

"So nice to meet you," he said shaking their hands.

And to Hannah he said, "Mike and I will do our best to bring him home." Then he paused. "What year is this?"

It was a difficult answer to give to a friend, but I told him the truth.

"You're quite a few years into the future. We are now in the 1990s," I replied.

He spent a few minutes gasping and trying to breathe. Hannah, apparently ready for this or something like it, handed him a shot of one of Westlake's whiskeys. He drank it, and after a moment he stopped hyperventilating and became Jim again.

"There are many things I would ask you, including things about me, but I guess I'd rather discover them for myself." Then he said, "I hated the fucking sixties."

We then got to the business at hand and Jim was all over it. It turned out that his father really was a rear admiral (look it up) and that Jim had more than a passing acquaintance with all manner of weapons. He'd fired hand guns, machine guns, and even anti-aircraft guns from the deck of his dad's aircraft carrier, and all by the time he was a teenager. He knew military protocol inside and out so I would be following his lead.

As we picked through the extensive wardrobe room of the mansion, a collection of clothes and outfits from many eras and places that would make a Hollywood set designer jealous, Jim's plan started to take shape.

"This'll do," he said as he found a WWII US Army Major's uniform that fit him nicely, along with a matching helmet. Hannah looked to Jim and said, "What's the plan?"

"Mike will be my attaché," he said. "It literally means 'attached' and Mike you have to take that very seriously. Stay at my side and let me do all the talking. I know how these guys think."

As rock fans, many of us had seen the brilliance of an almost always stoned Jim Morrison. I was now seeing him mostly sober, and totally focused. He was a natural born leader, and on stage, his vision became his reality, and millions of us got on board and followed. As I would do now, even with my life at stake.

So I would once again be reprising my role as the quiet associate, but I was ok with it as I had no concept of military protocols. At least this time I was not portraying a stuttering killer like I ended up playing during our Grand Canyon adventure, or a temperamental hot head like I was during our Lewis and Clark episode. And maybe this time I wouldn't lose my hat...I mean...helmet.

****

I wore the outfit that Hannah had previously put together for me, and I looked official enough. Jim gave his approval and looked at my Walther P38 and said, "hmm...it's a German pistol, but I think it'll give you some cache, so that's cool."

Hannah brought Jim down to the firing range in the cellar and showed him the vast arsenal of weapons from all ages that Westlake had amassed. There were spears, bolos, tomahawks, long bows, muskets, and all forms of current and ancient projectile weapons. Jim chose a Thompson submachine gun and a .45 caliber Colt pistol. He was a child in a toy store.

"This is amazing! Where did Patrick get this shit?"

Hannah said that he was a historian who traveled extensively through time, and needed to fit into whatever scenarios he encountered. To Jim it was a revelation. He had been all about getting blasted and going somewhere. Now he saw ways to blend instead of stand out. He saw avenues where he could be a human just walking among humans.

We each shot off a few rounds at the targets set up along the other end of the room. I wasn't sure if I'd be able to pull the trigger if those targets were flesh and blood, but maybe no soldier ever knows that until the battle starts. Hopefully we'd be able to quickly locate Westlake and get him and us out of there without too much commotion, but we weren't kidding ourselves, we were heading into one of bloodiest battles of WWII. Jim asked if he could carry my Dad's Army picture. I thought it odd, but I gave it to him.

We went back upstairs and Hannah trimmed our hair. Jim had mentioned having a doctor there awaiting our return. Hannah said, "I called Dr. Collins. He said he'll be here shortly." He was the local Doc that Westlake paid handsomely to be discreet about the goings on at the mansion. Who knows what crazy shit he saw in his tenure with this time traveling couple? I just know he was never called for or needed in my time with them. Not till now.

Jim looked me over in my Army uniform as if he was a superior office conducting an inspection and nodded, but not without pointing to my helmet.

"Fasten that chinstrap," he said.

"It's not very comfortable," I replied.

"Are you quibbling, soldier?" he replied with a scowl. "Trust me."

I nodded and did what he 'ordered' even though it squeezed my face.

I brought Jim to the chair. He was confused by the need for it but then he was a man who didn't need ley lines to get where he wanted to go. We were supposedly going there to investigate the disappearance of an Associated Press reporter...a certain Brian Pedrick.

To hear from Hannah that Westlake had chosen a name combining the first and last names of my two best childhood friends, my early tree climbing spying compadres, Brian Farina and Stacey Pedrick, touched me no end...but then he was now family, so it shouldn't have surprised me.

Jim sat in the chair, I guess in deference to me. He did it with a comfortable arched eyebrow. Instead of annoying me, it made me feel safe. I would be traveling with an expert.

Before we left, I hugged Gin and she said, "Don't you dare not come back."

So that's what I kept in my head as I took my place behind the chair...and Boom, we were gone.

29

Ground Control to Major Jim

"Oft hope is born when all is forlorn."
J.R.R. Tolkien, *The Return of the King*

*"It's hard to lead a cavalry charge if you think you
look funny on a horse."*
Adlai Stevenson ll

We landed behind a tree, on the outskirts of Bastogne,
on the morning of December 22, 1944. It was snowy,
cold and foggy, and the town was in its second day of
being surrounded. Jim had chosen a spot in 'no man's
land' that was thankfully closer to Allied lines than
German.

There had been enough shelling that we could smell
it hanging in the air. The other smells were less pleasant.
It was probably burnt flesh and bodily fluids. Jim
immediately pushed me to the ground and said, "The
next few minutes are very important. Stay low and
follow me...and god dammit, buckle that chin strap!"

I did as he asked, but it kept coming unsnapped. We
kept low and worked our way from tree to tree in a
direction that Jim chose. We could hear a smattering of
gunfire in the distance, but thankfully nothing near us.
Suddenly a voice rang out.

"Tell me who you are or you're dead!"

We froze, or at least I did.

"I am Major James Morrison," Jim announced. "Like every other sad motherfucker in this area, I am retreating to Bastogne. Do you have a problem with that?"

We were now standing and I could see that we were covered by more than a few weapons aimed in our direction. I was trying to breathe, but Jim was irritated.

"Is this the way you treat an officer?" His stance awaited a response.

A Sergeant came closer, gun ready. "I don't know you from Adam's asshole and your buddy is carrying a German pistol. Now tell me what team Joe DiMaggio plays for!"

Jim paused for a moment, looked off into the distance, and said, "First of all my 'buddy' as you call him is my attaché, and he took that pistol off of a German soldier that he killed about an hour ago. Second of all, are you fucking kidding me? Are these the questions you're asking? Someone from fucking Siberia knows the answer to that."

The Sergeant shifted uncomfortably but wasn't backing down, "Answer the question."

We both clearly knew that the answer was the Yankees, but for whatever reason Jim was having none of it.

"No, you answer this question," he barked. "Who sang the vocal on Glen Miller's hit song *Chattanooga Choo Choo*?"

I was thinking we were about to get shot or arrested, but the Sergeant looked confused. He didn't know the answer.

"That would be Tex Beneke," Jim said, "Now either I'm going to have you arrested as a German spy, because you don't know that, or you're going to let us in."

The Sergeant slowly shook his head and started laughing, as did the other soldiers around him. "I'm sorry sir," he said. "We've had some issues with Germans dressed up like us."

"And I'm sorry for being an asshole," Jim replied. "I know you're just doing your job. Now can you point us to wherever the injured are housed? We are looking for a possibly injured AP reporter."

"We've had to keep moving them around, sir. And there's a lot of them," the Sergeant reported. "But Lewis here will take you to the nearest bivouac."

Lewis said, "Right this way, sir."

We followed.

"Jeezus Jim, Tex Beneke?" I said under my breath.

"Yup," Jim said with a smile.

We walked past numerous foxholes and make shift fortifications. Many of the soldiers were talking quietly, some were sleeping, and some were eating. Most of them looked exhausted. They'd been under almost constant fire for days. Lacking cold weather gear in the coldest European winter in years and running short on food, ammunition, medical supplies, and in some cases senior leadership, and outnumbered five to one they fought on. I sensed no quit in them; they were all in, and in their minds it was to the last man. I was humbled by their almost casual bravery. Many of these soldiers were part of, or attached to, the legendary 101 Airborne Division. After this battle they would earn the nick name *The Battered Bastards of Bastogne*.

In four days General George 'Blood and Guts' Patton would break through enemy lines and end the siege, but these men of course didn't know that. As I looked at each and every one of them, I was reminded of a discussion I had with Westlake many years prior...each and every one of these men were precious. Not one knew what their future held and quite a few were not going to make it home. I felt a wave of sadness come over me, but I pushed it to the back of my mind. Jim and I had a job to do.

We skirted an area of waist high weeds and came upon countless more soldiers in, or standing near, foxholes. Jim bent down as if to tie his boot and Lewis lit a cigarette. I noticed that Jim had my Dad's picture in his hand. Then he said so that only I could here, "Look about fifty feet over to your left but don't say anything, and don't go any closer. It wouldn't be a good idea."

And there, was my Dad. My legs went out from under me but Jim grabbed me before I hit the deck. "Battle fatigue," he said to Lewis, "Give him your canteen." Lewis handed me his canteen and I splashed some water on my face, which hid the fact that it was already wet.

As I caught my breath, I looked from under my helmet across at my Dad. He was standing over a foxhole talking seriously to the two men in it. He looked miserable. My Dad was always one to try and lighten up serious moments by being a wise ass. That's one of the things I inherited from him. As I looked at him now however, thirty years younger than me, I saw how distressed he was. Had I been able to walk any better at that moment, I might not have been able to heed Jim's advice about not getting closer but I couldn't help him and it crushed me. Jim patted my shoulder and half-smiled.

"Let's go," he said softly.

I nodded and we moved on in search of an injured friend. See ya' in a few years, Dad, I thought.

Then we heard a loud squeal and someone yelled, "Incoming!"

I got knocked sideways into a foxhole by either Jim or Lewis seconds before the world exploded. It probably saved my life. The war had started again.

30

Riders on the Storm

"You're braver than you believe, stronger than you seem, and smarter than you think."
Winnie the Pooh

"We'll never survive!" "
"Nonsense. You're only saying that because no one ever has."
William Goldman, *The Princess Bride*

I couldn't hear anything. I was face down in a hole and my head was ringing. I wasn't wounded but I'd lost my helmet. The ground around us was exploding, and there was nothing to do but hang on. I had a worried thought about my Dad, but then I remembered that he'd survived this. I was hoping to do the same but if I got punched out here, I was punched out for real.

There was a brief pause in the bombing, and I took a peek above the rim of the foxhole. The first thing I saw was my helmet, about ten feet away. It had a serious dent in it. It didn't seem like a good time to retrieve it, but I knew that the shrapnel that hit it would have ended me if I didn't have it on.

Jim was whacking me on the arm and saying something. The only word I recognized through lip reading was 'chinstrap'. My hearing came back abruptly, which shouldn't have been a big surprise...I'd seen Led Zeppelin in a small club in Boston in 1969, and my hearing survived that. My hearing was apparently pretty resilient.

"How many fingers am I holding up?" Jim asked.

"Blarga foo goba," I replied...before I gained control of my mouth.

Jim looked into my eyes and shook his head. "You might have a slight concussion. I told you to strap that helmet on tight."

"Sorry," was all I could mutter.

"Well, your language skills have suddenly returned. That's a positive." Jim then turned to Lewis. "We have to move. We're not here for this. Lead on Lewis."

We jumped up out of the foxhole and began quickly moving back in the direction we were originally heading. I took a look back at my Dad's foxhole, and at my dented helmet and then followed Jim at a quick pace. Lewis was still in the lead.

We made it about another fifty yards when we again heard, "Incoming!" We dove to cover and hugged the ground for ten minutes until the destruction ended. It was like a giant had eventually stopped pounding the earth. My head was screaming in pain like nothing I had ever experienced before. Jim was probably right about the concussion and I struggled to open my eyes once the shelling stopped.

"The Krauts will be coming now. They always come after the second shelling," Lewis explained. "The place I was taking you to is about a hundred yards that way. If you don't mind, sir, I should get back to my position."

"Well done, Lewis," Jim said. "Get back to your position."

Lewis nodded and left and we headed in the direction he'd indicated. We came to a place where there were a number of tents, sheds and all sorts of temporary facilities housing the wounded. It was an overall house of horrors. I won't go into details.

"There's thousands of wounded," I said to Jim. "How can we find him?" It seemed hopeless.

"Look for the sparkle," Jim replied.

Of course. I should have known that.

We ran through endless scenes of wounded and dying men, each one a hero with a story, but still we saw no Westlake. I was wondering how I would face Hannah if this didn't turn out right.

The last shed we came to in this stretch was lit with action. There were soldiers setting up to defend it while medics carried the wounded out the door and onto the waiting trucks.

Suddenly about two hundred yards away, we saw German soldiers advancing, some of them running, and quickly gaining ground on our position. The few soldiers defending the shed were outnumbered but they set up a furious enough response that the Germans were slowed.

We were going to keep moving on when we saw a very subdued sparkle coming from one of the carried patients. I rubbed my eyes to make sure it wasn't a side effect of the concussion I was suffering. Again the sparkle. It had to be Westlake. The fact that his sparkle was faint did not bode well, but at least we'd found him.

"Keep the shed between us and them," Jim yelled, as we ran towards the truck Westlake was being put in. Then Jim ran to the left of the shed, dropped and began firing. I realized he was buying me time. I got to the truck just as the driver was shot dead. I jumped in the back of the truck and found Patrick, head bandaged and unconscious. It was time for me to take him home.

I started the travel process, but then realized that Jim could die here too and I realized I couldn't leave a brother behind. Me, who'd never killed more than a mosquito, was heading into battle.

Damning myself and thinking we were fucked, I pulled my Walther and crept back toward the shed. I came up behind Jim.

Jim realized I was behind him and after bursting off some shots yelled, "Get the fuck out of here! And take him with you. I'll meet you on the ribbon."

That's what Jim called the Akashic strand that contained all of life's history...the ribbon.

I turned to get back to the truck when two German soldiers came around the right side of the shed. In the moment that they were surprised to see me, I shot one and he went down. The other was sure to kill me, but before he could lift his rifle, his middle exploded. Jim had taken him down with a burst of gunfire.

"Go!" he screamed as more Germans poured into the area. The last thing I heard before getting back into the truck was Jim unleashing a war cry that was more guttural and passionate than any rock star scream I'd ever heard.

I ran to the truck, stood next to my unconscious friend, and still hearing gunfire, and wondering if I'd ever see my other friend again. I took us out of there.

31

Break on Through
(To the Other Side)

"Lots of people want to ride with you in the limo, but what you want is someone who will take the bus with you when the limo breaks down."
Oprah Winfrey

"There are no happy endings, endings are the saddest part. So give me a happy middle, and a very happy start."
Shel Silverstein

We blinked out of Bastogne into the pale light of a billion stars, as if we were standing in outer space, though I was the only one standing, Westlake was horizontal. I reminded myself that Jim and I would have to support his weight before we grounded back at the mansion...that's if Jim made it.

I pictured our destination and got us close. Then I bumped away. That was the word Jim used to describe how he would avoid the harsh toll that being away from your own time for too long would extract from your body. Bumping your time repeatedly before finally arriving would gradually acclimate your body and greatly diminish the bad effects of extended time away. A quick arrival now would surely kill Westlake.

The only problem was that though I'd bumped before, it was always with Westlake doing the exercise and me along for the ride; except for once when he let me do the first two bumps. It takes a great deal of concentration to pull away from your landing spot at the last minute.

Jim had been tripping his brains out when he accidentally discovered the method. The drugs kept him initially from completing his return. But then with the single minded focus that LSD is sometimes able to deliver, he bumped against his own time five or six times before finally arriving. He was prepared for the worst but only had a mild headache.

My current situation was this: I would have to bump our mansion landing multiple times to even give Patrick a decent chance of survival...and I didn't have the skills and I was struggling to remain focused with the pounding in my head from the concussion I'd gotten during the shelling. It was one thing for a dedicated scientist who'd studied all aspects of time travel to bring us home...or for a genius poet and legendary rocker who was a 'human ley line' it once again would be easy...but I was a part time and wounded traveler, usually a passenger on someone else's trip, who only knew the basics.

I bumped our home place once again, and this time the pull away on my psyche was twice as hard. I wasn't sure I could do a third as I nearly blacked out. If I couldn't bump home and then pull away on the next one, whatever was left of Patrick would be in no shape to survive the return.

Where the hell was Jim?

I couldn't keep us out here forever. The ribbon might send you back where you just came from if you didn't act aggressively towards your next place. I had to try the third bump.

Patrick's eyes fluttered. It was the first movement of any kind I'd seen from him. I bent down and tapped his shoulder and said, "Here we go buddy."

I bumped us close and then began the pull away from the mansion but it wouldn't let me go. I tried with all my strength to get us away, but I was locked in a place inches away from home...a home I wasn't ready for yet.

I knew that in seconds I would be delivering a dead man to Hannah. I screamed in frustration.

"Good one," Jim said suddenly at my side. "You should start a band."

We were instantly heading back out to the middle ground of time travel. I felt a great release on my psyche. Jim knew my band had recently stopped playing, so it was his dig at me to keep playing.

He looked like hell. He was bleeding from his left shoulder, and it looked like he'd lost the little finger on his right hand.

"Jeezus, fuck are you ok?" I asked.

He had stopped the bleeding near his missing finger with a tourniquet at his wrist, but his shoulder was still bleeding.

"Well, I may never play the piano again," he said holding up his hand.

In spite of the most stressful moment of my life, I started laughing and so did Jim. It was stupidly funny, but also a perfect example of his grace under fire. He then effortlessly bumped us time after time while telling me what happened.

"I got lost in the moment. I should have left the second you blinked out, but the fucking Germans kept coming. I fired til I was empty. I got out a little too late. "

His shoulder was still bleeding and was now soaking his uniform.

"There's a doc waiting there for us. He'll fix you up," I said realizing that Jim needed help soon.

"I can't go there again, Mike, it's too far in the future. It's too fucking freaky. And besides, Patrick needs the doc more than me."

Seeing the amount of blood Jim was losing, I wasn't sure that was accurate.

"But where will you go?"

"Hold him up so he doesn't land hard," Jim said and I followed his orders one last time.

In his best train conductor voice Jim bellowed out, "Now landing on track nine, straight from Bastogne, all out at the Mansionnnnn!"

Then he blinked away...and Patrick and I were finally home. It seemed like it had been a lifetime ago that Hannah had come to our house in tears but it was only a couple of days in her and Gin's time. I don't know what happened to Jim...but then...first things first.

32

People are Strange
(and Wonderful)

"How did it get so late so soon?"
Dr. Seuss

"All we have to decide is what to do with the time that is given us."
Gandalf, *The Fellowship of the Rings* by J.R.R. Tolkien

It was a week later.

Patrick was sitting up in bed. He had a nasty scar above his right eyebrow but like all handsome people, it irritatingly only added to his 'look'. It had been touch and go for the first few hours of his return. Doctor Collins had done much tut tutting as he labored over Patrick but thankfully medicine and antibiotics had taken a great leap forward in the many years since that heinous war. Patrick had suffered a severe concussion, and some internal bleeding, but he would make a complete recovery.

We had landed, me trying to support his weight, right next to the chair. I remember Hannah's loud intake of breath when we appeared. My first thought was that damn, he's heavy and my knees hurt but then I realized he was still breathing. The doc was onto it immediately, and I rolled over onto my back in the warm sunshine of an Ipswich day. We had made it.

My other memory of our arrival was standing up and seeing my eight year old daughter Sara running towards me. She leaped into my arms and we hugged and I knew that though she hadn't seen the return, she must have picked up on the energy the adults were giving off. Then I saw Gin, and the complicated look she gave me. She had been in support of our dangerous undertaking to retrieve Patrick, but holding my daughter and looking at Gin, I realized it would probably be a while before I would time travel again. I nearly collapsed and just sat down and let out a long sigh. My head was ringing as the weight of everything that I'd just seen and done hit me at once. It took me a few days under Gin's loving care to start to feel normal...if I ever could again after this experience.

Now seeing Patrick days later awake and lucid, I sensed he was having the same thoughts about time travel looking at his pregnant Hannah. As it was, there would be some complications with these supposedly 'old' people having a child. Their choices would be to either claim that they adopted the child, or move someplace else, remove the makeup, and start again.

I know how it turned out, but that's a story for another day. Let's just say that at this moment, Patrick was not only fully aware of his mortality, maybe for the first time, but also aware of his responsibility to his incoming offspring.

"How did you get me back here?" he asked.

He knew that I wasn't talented enough, or had enough practice to bring a severely injured man back by myself. So I told him the whole story; about Hannah coming to get me, about realizing I needed help in retrieving him from Bastogne, about recruiting Jim at Gettysburg, and finally about our battle at the shed to get him away. The hard part was telling him about Jim's part of that battle...not his heroics nor his saving my life, and eventually Patrick's by jumping on the ribbon, but about the bloody mess of a man I'd last seen and the uncertainty I had about his survival.

We got quiet for a bit. "Damn," Patrick whispered.

We both knew that given our current situations, going to find Jim would at the very least have to be put on hold for a while.

So what did Patrick have to say about his investigation of my Dad's Battle of the Bulge experience?

"You remember that your Dad told me that he'd killed his buddy. His friend's name was William 'Billy' Reynolds. He was one of the few friends your Dad had that had made it all the way with him since North Africa."

I was imagining all the adventures, good and bad, that the two of them had survived in more than two years of war. They were likely closer than brothers. Patrick was getting to details I was hearing for the first time.

"They had a game they called 'low card' that they played often. It went like this; if there was beer to be bought, an order to be relayed, or a pretty girl to talk to, they would draw a card from the deck. Whoever got the low card won the honor of performing the task or chore. If it was getting to be the one to talk to the pretty girl, it was a win. If it was the one who got to buy the round of beers, it was a loss."

"The thing is, they also played it under battle conditions. Low card had to run for ammo, or relay an order, or be the first one out of the hole while the other laid down covering fire. Since it was common practice for German snipers to home in on places G.I.s were running from, this last one could be a deadly loss for the last one out of the foxhole."

My god! It was almost a form of Russian roulette they were playing but it was in an entirely democratic form.

"Your Dad outranked Billy, so the fact that he played the game at all says a lot about him. He could have ordered Billy to do all of it, or someone else. The fact that your Dad and Billy were pals made him sensitive to the idea that he was playing favorites so he apparently took on some of the tasks he could have ordered others to do."

There were some things that came naturally to my Dad. He was an exceptional pool player who once held his own against Jackie Gleason, the comedian/composer/actor, and great pool shooter who played Minnesota Fats in the movie classic, 'The Hustler.' My Dad was also a talented card player who won his share of large pots over the years. I could see him thinking of their low card game as just another gamble.

"When your Dad told me the story over beers that day I asked him if Billy was a good card player. 'He'll no,' he said, 'Billy didn't know a straight flush from a full house. It's why we kept the game simple.' Well it turns out that your Dad had marked the deck, so that he could tell by feel whether a card was low or not. He'd also marked a few of the high cards"

I was stunned. "My Dad was cheating? I don't believe it!"

"Yes, he was cheating, but not in the way you think. You see when it was the mundane stuff, like who got to talk to the girl, or who had to pay for the beer, or take a message to HQ, he saw to it that Billy won most of the time, but when the battles happened and bullets were flying it was your Dad who mostly won. Then he would loudly curse his rotten luck, and do whatever had to be done. He was trying to keep his friend from getting killed. "

"Wow," I said, thinking back to the sad man I'd seen near the foxhole.

"Well, they'd been using the same deck for over a year. Your dad had made tiny pinholes in some of the cards; a pinhole near the corner of a card meant it was a low card, a pinhole near the middle meant it was a high card.

Anyhow, on the day in question, they were under heavy fire, and given the order to pull back. Your dad wanted to be the last one out of the foxhole. He took the deck out of his pocket, spread the cards across a flat piece of wood they'd used to place their mess kits, and Billy pulled a card. It was a three. Great thought your Dad, Billy would be the first one out. So Mike ran his finger along the cards, felt a tiny bump near the middle of a card and thinking it was a high card, he turned it over. It was a two. The bump near the middle wasn't a pinhole, the cards were just old and worn.

Your Dad was now going to be first man out. There were men pulling back all along the front, with those who were stationary expected to provide covering fire to those who were retreating. Before Mike jumped out of the hole, he told Billy, 'we're going about fifty yards back. You wait til I yell your name before you start, which will mean I'm in a hole and I can cover you. You won't be the only one running and for Christ sakes don't run in a straight line.'

Then he left and found a spot and yelled Billy's name. Billy jumped out of the hole and took three running steps just as the shelling started. He probably should have hit the deck, but he ran sideways to a small clump of trees where a couple of other men were laying low.

The shelling was as heavy for the next ten minutes as anything the men had so far experienced. Your Dad had no choice but to hunker down. When the shelling stopped, the tree clump and the men behind it were nowhere to be seen. Your father tried to work his way over to the area, but the enemy fire was too intense. Then they were ordered once more to make a fighting withdrawal. He wouldn't be able to get back to that area again until Patton broke the siege a few days later.

When he returned, he found bodies and many indistinguishable body parts and some dog tags, but nothing of his friend. Near a bloody hole however, he found part of a playing card. It was a three. In his mind he should have been the last man out. It should have been him who died there. It should have been part of his card that was found."

"That's fucking bullshit! It wasn't his fault. He didn't kill him. That fucking war killed him." I was pretty upset.

"Very true," Patrick said. "But it's not for us to say who should or shouldn't feel guilty about something."

I calmed down, and got back to the story and asked this:

"So how did you get hurt, and what did you find out?"

Hannah was hovering. This was Patrick still recovering but she would say when he should stop. I was good with that.

"I showed up there right after a shelling. It was the day before you and Jim would arrive. I of course didn't know you were coming, but then if I'd come back you two wouldn't have needed to come and get me." He smiled at me. This was the way time travelers talked to each other. Anyone trying to follow along had to really pay attention.

"I was the AP reporter, Brian Pedrick, who, according to my credentials, had been along with the 101st Airborne for quite a while, but the operation was huge, so once you got back stage and looked the part, there were no questions asked. "

That resonated with me. Some people ended up back stage at Fools shows for the simple reason that they had a persona and great hair. The roadies thought, 'they must be someone.'

Patrick continued, "It was pretty common at the time; reporters, just like soldiers got stranded at

Bastogne. They gave me free reign to move about and I had some world class binoculars with me. They looked like items from that time period, but they were many optic levels above. My plan was to identify your Dad and Billy from a long ways off. I got to what I thought was a perfect viewing point, a small rise about three hundred yards back of the front lines in the area I thought was generally where your dad might be. I wasn't the only one there. There were spotters with radios relaying information to command posts.

I was early enough that I had time to search the trenches and foxholes. I found them as the battle restarted, both of them firing repeatedly at the approaching enemy. The Germans were about a half a mile away from me, so they were much closer to Allied lines. They were being shelled, but they were still coming like a wave. I saw your Dad leave the foxhole and run bent over before diving into another. He started firing just as Billy tried to retreat. I looked at the small clump of trees I knew he was going to head for, just as the shelling started. The shells were starting to make their way towards my little hill. The soldier next to me yelled 'get down' but I had to see what I came to see. The tree clump took a direct hit and became a smoking hole. No one could have survived it but as the smoke cleared, I saw a man crawling. He was pulling himself along and one of his legs wasn't helping. Then my world exploded, I had a dream that I was walking in outer space...and then I woke up here."

"But when my Dad got back there a few days later, he couldn't find any trace of Billy."

I pictured him turning over all sorts of ruined and disfigured humans in search of his friend. It was heartbreaking. My Dad got drunk that night and stole a general's jeep. He rolled it over at high speed and lived to tell the tale. He was busted back down to private.

"So that must have been him crawling! Maybe he somehow survived," I said. "But if he had, I'm sure my Dad could have found him among the wounded that were being cared for. What do you think happened?" I couldn't make any sense of it.

"I don't know, Mike," Patrick said. "But I should have added that the injured man wasn't crawling towards our lines, he was crawling towards the Germans."

33

The Unknown Soldier

"Five to one baby, one in five, no one here gets out alive."
Five To One by The Doors

"The best mirror is an old friend."
George Herbert

"He was just half blown up," I said. "I doubt he knew in which direction he was crawling. He was probably thinking something as simple as 'get away from the explosion.' Maybe he was taken prisoner?"

"He might have been, Mike, but the Germans were coming off a stretch where they weren't taking prisoners. A week before, and about forty miles away in Malmedy, some hundred American prisoners were brought to a field, to await transport to prison and or labor camps." He was now reading from notes he had made. "But on their way to other places, a Nazi SS unit commanded by Colonel Joachim Peiper happened upon the scene. He stopped his soldiers and had them take places along the field. He then ordered his soldiers to fire. Eighty-four of the prisoners were machine gunned to death, and the rest fled to escape into the woods. It became known as the Malmedy Massacre."

Incredibly, it was learned after the war that massacres committed by the Germans in most cases were not done by angry or enraged soldiers. The order had actually come down from the high command to stop taking prisoners, in hopes that it would spread fear among the Allies. It had the opposite effect.

The survivors told the story. After that, for better or ill, while many German soldiers were taken prisoner, sometimes by the thousands, SS soldiers were often taken to a nearby place and 'relocated,' a euphemism for a bullet to the head."

"But still, even if he crawled a ways before either dying or being executed, my Dad would've found him," I argued.

I was given the raised eyebrow look from Hannah as I asked this. Patrick was starting to look exhausted.

"If he lived through it, he was taken prisoner. Whatever happened after that, he may not have survived the war at a prison camp. You should go to the library and find out whatever you can. They still have the most extensive data base in town. Good luck, I hope you can find out that at the very least, he survived the war."

Westlake had a good computer, as did Gin and I, but the enormous reach of the World Wide Web was still a few years away. The library was a good choice for a number of reasons, the main ones being their access to not only thousands of newspaper files from around the globe, but also the resources of other libraries around the nation. Also, many librarians were top notch retrievers of information. Eleanor Adler was just such a person.

The next morning I got to the Ipswich library early. It's a classic old style library built in 1869 that exudes charm and character. Wall panels, shelves, and railings made of cherry and other hardwoods all burnished by more than a century of contact with human hands.

The main desk had the look and stature of a very wide podium. You were meant to stand behind it, not sit behind it, and that's where the head librarian was.

I hadn't seen her in almost twenty years, the last time I was in the place. Her name was Eleanor. At that time Westlake had given me a date in history and told me to discover what was special about it. I couldn't tell her I was curious about a random date and expect any help, so I told her the lie that it was the day my daughter was born and that someday I'd like to tell her what was happening on the day she was born.

Eleanor gave it her full attention and we discovered, after an extended search that mentioned riots, bombings, and other unhappy events from that day, a quirky fact that seemed like a fun thing to mention to a daughter; two men named Patterson and Gimlin had claimed to film a Bigfoot.

Though she was now probably close to retirement, Eleanor had aged well. She had been an attractive middle aged woman, and she was now a handsome elderly woman.

I walked up to the desk. She looked up from whatever she was doing and gave me a curious look.

"Back again?" she said.

I couldn't help but belt out a laugh.

"It's been too long," I said. She had a glint in her eye.

"How's the daughter?"

I didn't for a second think she was remembering my fascinating personality after all these years. She was apparently one of those rare people who are able to bring up past moments without trying.

"My daughter is twenty years older and still the apple of my eye. It's good to be back in this great old place."

"And what are we looking for this time," she said dryly.

I liked this woman.

There seemed no reason to lie this time. I told her my Dad's story, in a shorter form, but she got the gravity of it. She asked me questions, and I told her what I knew, which wasn't much. My Dad had told Westlake that Billy Reynolds was from California. For a kid from Ipswich in the 1940's, California must have seemed like the other end of the universe. The only other thing I knew was that he might have been captured at the Battle of the Bulge.

Eleanor started digging into not only Army records, but California veterans' info and European war records. I had no part in it except to sit next to her and listen to the noises she made as she searched.

When she groaned I felt despair, but when she said 'hmmm' with an uplifting lilt, I felt hope. It went on for a couple of hours. But then she said this:

"I've got him! That fucker lived!"

I was stunned by the revelation but almost more by hearing a librarian swear in a library! But the important news was this: Billy survived the war!

34

Deuces Wild

"You don't drown by falling in water, you drown by staying there."
Edwin Louis Cole

"Life isn't fair, it's just fairer than death, that's all."
William Goldman, *The Princess Bride*

I drove right back to the mansion, pretty much ignoring the local speed limit. I found Westlake up and walking. His conditioning and regimen were such that it probably had him recovering at a faster rate than most humans, but it was still impressive, considering his injuries.

I excitedly told him and Hannah about what I'd learned. William 'Billy' Reynolds indeed had the very good fortune to be taken prisoner that day outside of Bastogne. Lucky for him there were still some German officers willing to play by the rules. He spent the rest of the war in a prison camp, and it was there that his right leg was removed. He was once again lucky, as most qualified doctors were at one military front or another.

Like most prisoners held by the Germans in the latter stages of the war, he was on a near starvation diet and was malnourished by war's end in May of 1945...but he was alive.

Upon returning from the war, he moved to San Diego, married, and had children...and grandchildren. It was a story like countless others of the returning veterans.

My Dad believed his best friend had died, and he believed it was his negligence, not his friend's, that had caused it. From the moment he returned to Ipswich, he shut off all connections with anything Army related. He also instructed my mother that if anyone ever called looking for him from his war days, to claim there was no one there by that name. If Billy had tried to reach him, my mother may have answered and did exactly as Dad instructed. One important fact would have made it difficult for Billy to locate my Dad. To all of his Army buddies, he was Mike Girard, but his real name was Francis Mark Girard, a name he never liked, and was embarrassed by.

There were few ways to track Army buddies after the war back then, but if he'd read any of the many newsletters sent to him by different veteran organizations, instead of tearing them up, he might have learned that William Reynolds had become an advocate for crippled veterans.

"Wow," Hannah said. "That's the best possible news! Well done, Mike."

"It wasn't me, thank Eleanor at the library." I made a mental note to have flowers sent to her on behalf of my family.

"It just remains now to tell my Dad," I said. There was only one person to do it. I looked at Patrick and he nodded.

****

According to Patrick, my Dad initially refused to believe it. Patrick's story was that while visiting San Diego on business, he happened to see a WWII vet on TV whose name was William 'Billy' Reynolds. He was speaking about crippled and severely injured veterans from America's wars, and saying that we as a country should feel shame at our neglect of the needs of these heroes.

Patrick claimed that he sought out the man, and asked if he was the Billy Reynolds who knew Mike Girard. (Patrick did do a short time travel and do precisely that, so as to solidify the tale)

But it wasn't until he showed my Dad a current picture of the old vet that my Dad tearfully exclaimed, "son of a bitch. That's Billy!"

The next few weeks were about working out the best way to bring these two old soldiers together. My sisters, Patti and Debbie, are great at organizing trips, so it was left for them to set it up. It turned out that for a number of reasons, one of them being Billy's health, that my Dad was on his way to San Diego. I couldn't make the trip (because the band had gotten back together and well...that's all in my other book), but my brother John did.

He sent me a picture of two old men, smiling and arm in arm, each holding a playing card. They were both holding twos.

EPILOGUE

With the encouragement of friends, family, and fellow time travelers, we Fools got back together. We are still together all these years later. I honor the gift of the Lady of Light, the mother of creation that made us all. That's how I see it.

In 2004, my brother John and I had the great pleasure of taking my Dad to the then recently created World War II memorial in Washington, D.C. He was a very old man and though he wanted to walk, we eventually pushed him around in a wheel chair. We were there on Memorial Day and he had his Veterans of Foreign Wars hat on. As we pushed him around, we felt like we were escorting a rock star as so many people thanked the old man for his service.

There are large carved stones around the expanse of the memorial there to commemorate one or another battle. We pushed my Dad through the crowd, which parted instantly as they saw him, an ancient warrior. When we got to the large carved stone that said Ardennes, my Dad gave a look that said 'leave me alone for a while.' We did. In some ways it was the best moment I ever spent with my Dad.

It was not a happy ending for everyone. On July 14, 1976, (Bastille Day) Joachim Peiper, the man who had ordered the Malmedy massacre, and who had seemed to skate through the post war trials was found murdered in his house. He was then living in France.

Whoever killed him also burned his house to the ground. There were a number of suspected killers, but the list, involving candidates from more than one country, might have been too extensive to investigate.

Patrick and Hannah moved to another place to have their baby. He's a fine healthy young fellow. Gin and I try and fly out to visit them as often as we can, but over time it's less frequent. It's hard for them to come back east given their history.

Rich Bartlett is now dating Eleanor Adler, the Ipswich librarian. They're a fun couple.

Patrick and I still occasionally time travel. We play it safe and go for what we think are easy quests...but it doesn't always play out that way.

I got a curious package in the mail a few years after the events of this book. There was no return address. In it were three things; the hat I sold at Gettysburg , the dented helmet I lost at The Bulge, and what looks like a golfing glove with the little finger cut off.
I guess Jim is still out there...at least I hope so.

Westlake's mansion was bought by the Catholic Church. Rumor has it that some strange visions have been experienced near the fountain. The Catholic jury is still out on what took place.

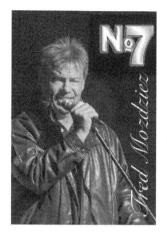

Sadly, Fred, my good friend, traveling partner and the 7th best roadie we Fools ever had, passed away in 2015. To anyone who ever met him, Fred was a special guy. He listened, he counseled, and he comforted so many people. It was not uncommon during and after show autograph session for people to ask for a Fred autograph. He became a band celebrity to our fans for his introduction of us.

"Ladies and gentlemen, from Ipswich Massachusetts, entertainment capital of the world, and home of the fried clam, please welcome...The Fooooools!"

No one has since taken Fred's place. No one will.

Cin-Cin, Freddie.

ACKNOWLEDGEMENTS

Nothing happens in a vacuum, except maybe time travel. The following people were instrumental in helping me bring about the creation of this story. My team of dedicated proof readers suffered through my many misspellings and my overuse of parentheses (damn) and yes... ellipses. Thank you Ginny Rudis, Lisa Z, and Rick Kilbashian (Skillet).

As I wrote the story, I would send each chapter to Ginny, Lisa, my musical partner in crime all these years, Rich Bartlett, and of course my friend and writing coach Lloyd Corricelli. It was with the encouragement and support of these people that I was able to take the many steps that made up the creative journey. Lloyd in particular is the reason I initially started writing and he, as an author, was invaluable in keeping me focused on the process.

Lloyd is one of the more fascinating people you'll meet. A world traveler who, in his spare time, has become a martial arts expert, plays guitar and sings behind his original rock tunes, and somehow finds time to write some excellent crime novels. That's also his handiwork on the back cover. Thank you, Lloyd! You can find Lloyd at www.authorlloyd.com.

Thank you also to the amazing Daniel Batal for his work on the cover. He made my story come to life. It turns out that he's not just a talented bass player, but a man

with some serious graphic skills. You can find him at
www.danielbatal.com.

And finally, it's sometimes difficult to write about a
departed loved one, in this case my Dad, without
running it by other relatives for their stamps of
approval. I'm happy to say that both my brother, John
Girard, and my sister, Patti Comeau Simonson, were
both understanding and supportive of the way I chose
to tell the story.

I am blessed to be surrounded by a loving group of
family and friends. I love you all.

ABOUT THE AUTHOR

Mike really did grow up in Ipswich, MA, really did tour the world as a member of the rock band The Fools and really does have a wife named Ginny and daughter named Sara. Everything else in-between is pretty much open to his interpretation of the events.

Mike enjoys playing video games, is an avid fan of cryptozoology, and loves to play with his daughter's German Shepherd Stella and his cat Monkey.

Mike has authored two books. This one and "Psycho Chicken and Other Foolish Tales;" the sort of true story of his band The Fools.

Made in the USA
Lexington, KY
12 November 2019